THE BROTHERS BROWN & GRAY

A Boston Detective Novel

GARY GLASS

Black Rose Writing | Texas

©2022 by Gary Glass
All rights reserved. No part of this book may be reproduced, stored in a retrieval system or
transmitted in any form or by any means without the prior written permission of the
publishers, except by a reviewer who may quote brief passages in a review to be printed in a
newspaper, magazine or journal.

The author grants the final approval for this literary material.

First printing

This is a work of fiction. Names, characters, businesses, places, events, and incidents are
either the products of the author's imagination or used in a fictitious manner. Any
resemblance to actual persons, living or dead, or actual events is purely coincidental.

ISBN: 978-1-68513-064-0
PUBLISHED BY BLACK ROSE WRITING
www.blackrosewriting.com

Printed in the United States of America
Suggested Retail Price (SRP) $21.95

The Brothers Brown and Gray is printed in Baskerville

*As a planet-friendly publisher, Black Rose Writing does its best to eliminate unnecessary waste to
reduce paper usage and energy costs, while never compromising the reading experience. As a result,
the final word count vs. page count may not meet common expectations.

For Elizabeth, always.

THE BROTHERS BROWN & GRAY

Part One. Gray.

PART TWO. BROWN.

*O the puzzle — the thrice-tied knot — the deep and dark pool! O all
untied and illumin'd!*
O to speed where there is space enough and air enough at last!
*O to be absolv'd from previous ties and conventions — I from mine,
and you from yours!*
O to find a new unthought-of nonchalance with the best of nature!
O to have the gag remov'd from one's mouth!
O to have the feeling, to-day or any day, I am sufficient as I am!

~ Walt Whitman, from "One Hour to Madness and Joy"

Part One. Gray.

CHAPTER 1

THE CREATIVE

First impressions can be deceiving, but when your first contact with someone is a 2:00 a.m. phone call it's hard not to assume right off that you're dealing with a horse's ass. McBride was sitting on the back porch, debating with the second half of a bottle of Malbec whether he ought to go to bed before dawn for a change. The spectral glow of a waxing moon seeped through the chilly air above the lake. Lonely bullfrogs bellowed for love. A crow cawed on a withered branch.

The phone buzzed on the table beside him. He jumped and snatched it up. No name. Boston area code. The time clicked over from 01:59 to 02:00 as he looked at it. One produces two, two plus two is four, measuring the marigolds. McBride slapped it back down and tapped it on speaker. It lay on a volume of Plotinus which he had been reading earlier in the evening.

"Who is this?"

"Morris Gray."

He reached automatically for the black Moleskine notebook and black Cross pen also on the table, flipped the book open where it was ribboned and started making notes: *0200 Morris Gray.*

"Who's Morris Gray?"

"A man who wants to hire you." Gray answered as quick as if he got that question all the time.

"You want to hire me?"

"Yes, can you come over?"

"At two in the morning?"

"Yes."

"At two in the fucking morning?"

"Yes." Gray sounded impatient. "I'll pay you."

McBride made a note: *in a hurry.* "Where?"

"The Taj in Boston."

"Ask Sylvia why she didn't invite me to the party." McBride looked across the water at her place — his partner's — sort of — the way a cat is your partner keeping mice out of the kitchen — if it's in the mood. No lights on. The lake was smooth as a mirror reflecting the cloudless night sky. My God, it's full of stars!

"Who is Sylvia?" — Not "Who's Sylvia," but "Who is Sylvia."

"Or is this supposed to be the invitation?" McBride said.

"What?" Off script now, Gray wasn't responding as quick. Sylvia's friends were usually sharper than this. But it was late — they'd already dismissed several bottles.

"Tell her I said it's not cute."

"There's no Sylvia here." Funny accent the asshat was affecting. Not local or generic midwestern. How do you pronounce M-e-d-f-o-r-d. One of her actor friends. Probably thought it sounded Forties or something.

"Either put her on or hang up, Morris."

"I said there's no Sylvia here, Mr. McBride." He sounded annoyed now.

"You're boring me, Morris. Repeating yourself. Bye-bye now."

McBride tapped him off, struck out his notes, and took another look at the Malbec. Fucking Sylvia. Always checking on me. Sweet girl, really. Like a forest cobra.

The phone buzzed again. Same number, of course. He let it lay there thrashing on the table like a dying hornet while he poured another glass.

It rolled over to voicemail.

He took a drink. The bullfrogs were really in fine voice tonight. Like beating fifty empty paint cans with fifty rubber mallets.

A minute passed before the hornet started thrashing again.

McBride tapped it on speaker. "It wasn't funny the first goddamn time."

"Mr. McBride, this is not a joke. I have a job for you. I need you to find someone."

He couldn't help himself, he wanted to know what the punch line was. Besides, it wasn't like he was busy.

"OK, who do you want to find?"

"That's as much as I care to say on the phone. Please come to the hotel. I'll pay you for your time."

"How much?"

"One thousand dollars."

"Nice round number. What's your room number at 'the Taj,' 'Morris'?"

"Eight oh eight."

McBride hung up and looked up the number of the Taj. They answered on the first ring. Two in the morning. He asked for room 808. Gray answered on the first ring too.

"Yes?"

"This is McBride. Who are you?"

"Morris Gray. Are you coming or not?"

"A thousand in cash? I don't do credit cards."

"I don't either."

"Who carries a thousand cash in their pocket?"

"It's in the room safe."

OK, that was quick. "Meet me in the bar."

"No, come to my room."

"Why?"

"Why not?"

"Who else is there?"

"No one."

"Who do you know that I know?"

"No one."

McBride took a drink and mulled.

Gray didn't let him mull long. "How soon can you be here?"

What the hell. "Well, you know how the traffic is before dawn. Thirty minutes."

"I'll tell the desk to let you up."

CHAPTER 2

THE RECEPTIVE

To strap or not to strap, that was the question. Two in the morning, unknown contact. But it was at the Taj, and, even after nearly thirty years of licensed gun use, packing still made him feel like a target. Contrary to gospel in certain circles, guns *attract* trouble. That's why bad guys carry.

McBride took his time getting dressed, took his time on the drive. At that hour 93 South was relatively empty, but he took his time anyway, enjoying the cool air and the smooth black road. He didn't make it in 30 minutes, and he didn't plan to. If Gray knew where he lived, then he'd know he wasn't likely to be there in 30 minutes. If Gray didn't take any notice of him being late, it could mean Gray was local and knew better. Or vice versa. Or not. But it was a data point. Anyway, it was generally a good idea not to be on time to any meeting where the other party had the advantage. Early was better than late, but late was better than predictable.

He parked on Newbury Street and walked around to the main entrance and went in to the front desk. The clerk looked like a door greeter from a Rodeo Drive boutique — skinny build, narrow chin, big brown mare eyes, all his hoarfrosty hair standing on top of his head.

"Evening," McBride said, answering the clerk's unimpressed frown with a big smile. "I'm Christian McBride, here to see Mr. Morris Gray. Room 808. He's expecting me."

"Yes, sir, Mr. McBride," said the desk clerk evenly, not cracking his frown, "you may go up." He sounded the part too — curled lip, art school condescension. "The elevators are just—"

"What's he like, this Morris Gray?" McBride rounded his shoulders and made his expression awkward.

The desk clerk's eyelids fell to half mast.

"You've met him, haven't you?" McBride said. "I don't know him." He huffed slightly. "The agency sent me." He shrugged. "Does he seem clean to you?"

The desk clerk's lips flirted with a snarl. "Mr. Gray is a very respectable guest, *Mister* McBride."

"Sure," McBride responded quickly. "Sure, but, *you know* … Is he *reliable?*"

Full snarl mode now, cold as ice: "No, I don't know."

That was enough. Desk clerk knew him, hadn't had any trouble with him, and didn't want any. Another data point.

McBride thanked him and went up.

.   .   .

He paused outside 808 and listened. No TV, no music, no voices. He knocked three times, not too hard, and stepped back from the door. Four seconds, he heard him walking up, heavy tread, heard the silence as he peepholed him, heard him unlock the door *and* throw back the latch. But the door didn't open.

Three seconds, then from inside, "Come in!" Muffled, like he'd backed away into the room.

McBride hesitated. Then knocked again. Three times, harder, as if he hadn't heard anything.

"Come in!" Louder.

"Open the fucking door, *Morris*."

Three seconds. Five. Ten. Life is short, regret is long. McBride was about to call it a night when the door handle turned down.

The door opened to shoulder width. Gray looked about 45, six foot even, 200 pounds, white, short fine light brown hair going grey, clean shaven, and naked as a statue — hairy chest, pasty skin, square build getting flabby, uncircumcised cock. Your standard issue business traveler, jet lagged and bored.

McBride almost laughed. The joke was on him after all. "Get the fuck out of here."

Gray managed to look genuinely confused. "What?"

McBride looked past him. Who else was in the room?

Gray stepped back, holding the door open. "Come in, please."

McBride didn't move. "Who else you got in there?"

"No one. Come in, please." Gray was uneasy. Data point.

McBride didn't move. "Forget your pants, Morris?"

"Are you coming in or not?"

McBride stepped forward, put his hand on the door, gestured with his nose. "You go ahead, I got the door."

Gray turned away impatiently.

It was a big room for a hotel, and McBride could see most of it from the door. Heavy-duty hotel furniture, but expensively upholstered. Big windows, curtains drawn. And aside from the middle-aged naked business traveler planted dead center, unoccupied.

McBride stepped inside and let the door close gently behind him. Gray waited till it snugged to, then without smiling put his hand out tentatively. He had an uncertain handshake, like he wasn't used to letting anyone touch his mitt. Everything about him seemed uncertain. He wasn't sure how to play his role. McBride decided not to help him out — Gray was the one who'd decided to play it in the raw.

"You're late."

Data point. McBride shrugged. "Traffic."

"It's important to me that you be punctual."

"I'll make a note."

There were two Edwardian chairs either side of a round mahogany table and a small sofa arranged opposite. White hotel towels covered the seats of both chairs but not the sofa. Gray planted his bare ass on one of the chairs.

McBride plucked the towel off the other and sat down. The seat was cool, thank god.

Gray leaned back and crossed one knobby bare knee over the other. "Now then," he said, and it was a complete sentence. "I want you to find my brother."

McBride pulled the notebook from his jacket, flipped it open to the ribbon marker, wrote "stet" next to the notes he'd crossed out before. "Who's your brother?"

"I don't know his name."

"You don't know your brother's name?"

"I didn't even know I had a brother until recently."

"Separated at birth?"

"Yes." Like he didn't know it was a joke.

"Why?"

"We were adopted."

"Why?"

"I don't know."

"Why do you want to find him?"

"Because he's my brother."

"How do you know you were adopted?"

"I deduced it. And when I challenged my parents they admitted it."

"But they didn't tell you about the brother?"

"No. They didn't know."

"How do you know they didn't know?"

"Because they didn't tell me."

"How old were you when you figured it out?"

"Fifteen."

"What tipped you off?"

"I didn't look like them."

"What are your adoptive parents' names?"

"They're dead."

"What are your *dead* adoptive parents' names?"

"Anderson and Margaret Gray."

"Mother's maiden name?"

"Hornecki."

"Spelling?"

"What difference does it make?"

"H, O, R, N, E, … am I getting warm?"

"Are you what?"

"Spell it."

Gray heaved a sigh and spelled it out, letter by offended letter.

"When did they die?"

"We're wasting time."

"I haven't been here five minutes."

Morris uncrossed his legs and let his foot flop to the floor. He was probably right-handed. Most people cross their dominant side over their nondominant.

"Why do you need all these details about my parents?"

"What about your natural parents?"

"I don't know anything about them."

"Not curious?"

"No."

"But you are curious about your brother."

"Yes."

"Why?"

"What difference does it make?"

"It makes a difference to me."

"Why, are we also related?" Gray thought that was cute. He smiled a self-satisfied little smile.

McBride didn't. "You're supposed to ask me if I'll take your case."

"Why wouldn't you?"

"Because I don't like you."

"I'm not asking you to make love to me." Cuter still.

"And you're supposed to ask me if I'm up to the job. Don't you want to know my qualifications?"

"No."

"Twenty years Boston PD. Fifteen detective. Six years private practice."

"That's fine."

"Why me then?"

"For this investigation, do you mean?"

"Yes do I mean. You just happen to pick my name out of the private dick directory at two in the fucking a.m.?"

Gray hesitated.

McBride waited. He wasn't going to let him dodge this one.

After he'd had a few seconds to think about it, Gray finally offered, "You were recommended."

Not good enough. "By who?"

"I prefer not to say."

"Too bad."

"I can't say."

"Why not?"

Gray clamped his flabby character-actor lips together, watched McBride watching him. The seconds clicked past. McBride started thinking about asking for the grand.

"Well!" Gray said suddenly and heaved himself to his feet. "I have been teaching myself to make martinis. Would you like one? I'm having one." He turned toward the console bar against the wall. "I've been trying different flavors of gin. My current favorite is No. 3 London Dry. I haven't tried One or Two yet." Over his shoulder: "Or perhaps you're a vodka man?"

"Gin."

"I suppose you take it tough."

"Tough?"

"Extra dry."

"Classic."

"Clean or dirty?"

"Clean."

"Garnish?"

"As you like."

"Rocks or straight?"

"Neat."

"Neat. Right." Like he'd just learned a new word.

"Shaken not stirred?" Back to the cute.

"Bond was a spy, not a dick."

"Double-O-seven."

"Nick Charles is your man."

"Who?"

"The Thin Man."

"Dashiell Hammett, right."

McBride watched Gray's backside jiggle as he shook the mix. He didn't look like he got much exercise. Or much sun.

Gray took martini glasses out of the mini-fridge under the bar.

"How long have you been in Boston?" McBride said.

"A few months."

"Where are you from?"

"New York."

"When did you find out about the brother?"

"That's why I came here," he said, turning round. He crossed back, his ridiculous dick swinging between two perfectly beautiful double martinis. He handed McBride the one in his right, then pointed with the same hand at a blank sheet of paper lying on the table between their chairs. "Look at that."

McBride took a sip of the drink, and hissed in through his teeth.

"That's damn good actually."

"Thanks." He carried his drink back to his side of the table and sat back down on his towel.

McBride set the glass down on the table and turned the paper over. It was a grainy grayscale picture of a hockey game. Actually just two players, near the corner boards, one of them legs apart, bent forward over the puck, the other his mirror image vaulting over him — back to back, legs making an X in the air, sticks at crazy angles. The flyer was going to come down hard. The one with skates still on the ice was a Bruin. You could see through the glass three first-row spectators caught in mid amazement: two females, who were probably pretty if not for the lousy picture and the glare on the glass, and a male between them — Gray's double. Different hairstyle, and wearing clothes, but the facial features were identical.

"Hockey fan?" McBride said, but he already knew who it was.

"I had never seen a hockey game before someone sent that photo to me."

"When?"

"Five months ago."

"In e-mail?"

"No."

"To your apartment?"

"I didn't say I had an apartment."

Good catch. Gray was an eccentric bastard, but he wasn't slow. And he made a hell of a martini.

"I don't have a fixed address. I live in hotels. Someone left it at the desk for me."

"In New York?"

"Yes."

"What hotel?"

"Different ones. I move around."

"What was the last one?"

"What difference does it make?"

McBride affected an Edward G. Robinson accent. "The way this works, see, is I asks the questions, and you makes the answers."

"You're wasting time asking me irrelevant questions."

"I'm not. I'm on the clock."

Gray hesitated, took a hit off the martini, deciding whether to answer, or what to answer: "The Marriott Essex."

McBride caught Gray stalling, so he drilled his questions rapidly, pressing him, looking for mistakes: "I don't know New York hotels. Where is that?"

"I don't know the address. South of Central Park. You can look it up." Not "South Central Park." Data point.

"What dates were you there?"

"I don't know. A year or more. Up until five months ago."

"Less than two years?"

"Yes."

"What do you do for a living?"

"I'm rich."

"How did you get to be rich?"

"My father made money in the computer business."

"Business name?"

"Different ones. He invested. Mostly in electronics parts, I think. I didn't know much about it. Why aren't you asking me about my brother?"

"What do you know about him?"

Gray decided to affect exasperation. Or maybe it was genuine. "Nothing about him. That's why I called you."

McBride picked up the picture again. "Was there any note?"

"No."

"Was it in an envelope?"

"No."

"Night clerk or day clerk?"

"Day."

"Man or woman?"

"The desk clerk? A woman."

"Name?"

"I haven't a clue."

"You were there over a year."

"Yes."

"Was she pretty?"

"Yes."

"Over a year and you never tried to hit that pretty little thing?"

"Why in the name of God would I want to hit anyone?"

"I want to hit someone most days. Though not generally in the name of God. Did she say anything about the person who dropped it off?"

"She said it was a courier."

"What service?"

"I have no idea."

"It hasn't been folded."

"So?"

"Is this the original?"

"It's a copy."

"Can I see the original?"

Gray was mildly surprised, then mildly amused. "No."

"Why not?"

"It's all I have. It's the only thing I own. Nobody sees it."

"The only thing you own?"

"Yes."

"You own some gin."

"Consumables don't count."

"You own any underwear?"

"Does nudity make you uncomfortable?"

"Not on the right people. Did you get any calls that day or the next, the day you got the picture?"

"No."

"Nothing? No voicemails? No hang-ups? No suspicious silences?"

"No."

"Do you have a birth certificate?"

"No."

"Why not?"

"I don't know. I've never had one."

"Where were you born?"

"Phoenix, Arizona."

"Where do your parents live now?"

"I told you they're both dead." Dodged a trick there.

"Their most recent place of residence?"

"I don't know. It's been thirty years since I last saw them."

"Why?"

"Because they weren't my parents."

"Hit you hard, finding that out."

"I suppose so."

"But they left you the money anyway."

"I was their only child."

"Did you hate them?"

"No."

"Did they hate you?"

"No."

"How do you know they're dead?"

"Their attorney contacted me."

"How did he find you?"

"I don't know."

"Did he call you?"

"He left a message."

"At the desk."

"Yes."

"How did you get the money?"

"Wire transfer."

"To your bank?"

"Yes."

"What bank?"

"I don't know. I have many bank accounts."

"What year was this?"

"About eight years ago."

"About? You're not sure about a thing like that?"

"No."

"How did they die?"

"No idea."

"Did they die together?"

"No idea."

McBride sat back, took a bite off his martini, and studied Gray. Gray tapped the nail of his right middle finger against the stem of his martini glass, impatient and nervous. Paranoid. After a minute, McBride settled his glass back on the table and picked up the notebook again, doggedly, for effect.

"Where did you get your accent?"

"What accent?"

"Have you ever traveled abroad?"

"No."

"Never?"

"I don't travel."

"How did you get here from New York?"

"I hired a driver."

"You came here to find him?" (Indicating the photo.)

"Yes."

"On the strength of the Bruins jersey on the player in the photo."

"Yes."

"What about the other player?"

"The fans are wearing Bruins shirts too."

"Good eye."

"Thank you."

"So what have you been doing to find him for the last five months?"

"Going to hockey games."

"Anything else?"

"No."

"Don't want to find him real bad, do you?"

"I've been busy."

"Doing what?"

"That's personal."

"Personal?" Then he decided to let it go. For now. "So what made you decide to engage a professional?"

"The season is almost over."

McBride pretended to study his notes for a minute, sipped his drink, tapped his nose with his pen.

"So the situation is this," he said, without looking up. "You learned five months ago that you have a twin brother. You don't know his name, your real parents' names, his adoptive parents' names, his place of residence, or anything else about him, except that he looks like you."

"And he likes hockey."

"And women." McBride pondered the matter professionally, like a plumber contemplating a busted bathtub. "All right, Mr. Gray, I'll take the case."

"I'm glad." Gray smiled — more relieved than pleased.

"But it won't be easy. And I'm not cheap." This was boilerplate. And the first part was probably even true.

"I understand."

"Chances are I'll never find the guy. For all we know he was here from out of town too."

"I understand."

"I still want the grand up front." This was just to annoy him.

"Of course," Gray said. "I have a few restrictions I will need you to abide by." Gray suddenly looked more serious than he had any time since McBride arrived.

McBride didn't like it. "And what would they be?"

"*Complete* confidentiality. You must work on the case alone. You must never discuss the case with anyone but me. Never. No matter how it comes out. Not even in the abstract. You must keep no records. Whatever notes you make you must turn over to me when you're finished. You must keep no copies."

"Why?"

"Also I will pay you only in cash. You must not report the income on your taxes."

"Uh-huh." This was getting riper every minute.

"I want you to report to me every day in person here in my room at two a.m. sharp. I have also purchased disposable phones for us. In an emergency, but only in an emergency, you may call me on my phone, but only on my phone, not the hotel phone, and only from your phone, the one I give you. Every call you make that is in any way connected to the investigation must be made using that phone. When our business is finished, you will return your phone to me. I have also purchased a laptop computer for you to use in the same way. And you must return it to me when you're finished."

"That's a lot of rules and regulations there, chief."

"It's necessary."

"Why?"

"I can't explain."

"Go ahead and try."

"It has to be this way."

"It's starting to sound like you're either crazy or dangerous. Probably both."

"I will pay you one thousand dollars a day, seven days a week, provided you work on my case exclusively."

"Which is it then, crazy or dangerous?"

"Time is of the essence, Mr. McBride."

"Is it? Why did you blow five months going to hockey games?"

"It's of the essence now."

"Why? What changed?"

"I'm going to die." He didn't say it like it was keeping him up nights.

"Of what?"

"I don't know yet. I have a premonition."

"So it's crazy." He made a note: *death wish.*

"If you succeed in finding my brother I will pay you a one-hundred-thousand-dollar bonus."

"And what am I to do when I find him?"

"Call me at once. Hopefully that is the only time you will ever call me. Do nothing else. Do not speak to him or approach him or reveal yourself in any way."

"Find and call. Got it. But I also have a few conditions. First, I want to see your ID."

Gray thought about it for a few seconds, decided to yield. He got up and went into the bedroom of his suite. McBride listened to him open the closet door, heard the safe chirp when he keyed in the combination, heard him sorting through the contents, heard it click back shut a minute later. Gray returned with a pillowcase hanging from his hand, looking like an out-of-work Santa Claus. He sat down and brought from the sack and handed across to McBride one by one a series of presents: a wad of Benjamins, a disposable mobile phone, a good-quality Sony laptop, and a beat-up blue US. passport. Then he tossed the empty bag into a corner of the room and padded back over to the bar and started cooking up another martini.

"I understand," he said over his shoulder, while McBride looked through the stuff, "you think I'm eccentric. I *am* eccentric. Unlike most people, I can afford to be. But that is real money in your hand."

Ten one-hundred-dollar bills crisp as autumn oak leaves. McBride tucked them into his pocket. The passport was seven years old. It was pretty beat up, but it had no stamps. He jotted the vitals from it into his notebook.

"Second condition," McBride said, "when we meet here every night at two a.m., wear some pants."

CHAPTER 3

DIFFICULTY AT THE BEGINNING

The first thing McBride did after rolling out of bed at noon was violate the terms of his hire.

"Sylvia, get your sweet ass over here."

"Good morning to you too, fuckhead."

"Seriously. I want to talk to you."

"I'll check my engagements."

"See you in ten."

Fifteen minutes later, emerging from the bathroom with his teeth brushed and his face wet, he heard her let herself in downstairs. He leaned over the rail and called down: "Can you put some coffee on, darling?"

She glared up at him from a baggy shirt and cargo shorts. "You call me that again, McBee, and I'll come up there and beat you senseless with the pot." It was like looking down at a coiled snake you'd just stepped on. That straight black hair and those unblinking brass eyes. What she looked at, she looked right at. He'd seen men twice her size — and twice as mean — back right down from that look. He and his ex had double-dated a few times with Sylvia and one or another of her exes. After they went to see Kill

Bill he took to calling her the unsung member of the Deadly Viper Assassination Squad, "Boston Timber Rattler," but it didn't stick. He had in fact seen her fight once. Quick, and neat, and very final. Remembering it made him a little uneasy.

"Just poison the coffee, slick. Less to clean up after."

"I'd enjoy it less."

He ducked into the bedroom to put his clothes back on. He could hear her banging around in the kitchen under his feet.

Sylvia yelled up: "You got a hot case?"

"Yeah!" he yelled back from inside his still-buttoned shirt, which he was pulling on over his head. "A case anyway. Hot, I don't know. But bizarre, moz def. Did you bring any food with you?"

"Scramble your own damn eggs."

He pounded down the stairs in bare feet, zipping his pants.

"So let's hear it," she said.

"I'm not supposed to talk about it."

"Then I'll listen extra carefully."

• • •

He told her the whole story while she unhelpfully watched him make himself breakfast (instant oatmeal and toast), poured coffee, and carried everything out to the porch. The weather had changed. A spring thunderstorm loomed. The heavy air pressed down, seemed to settle on the bent heads of the new grass scattered across his woody back yard. The lake was a lifeless grey sheet. The bullfrogs were sleeping it off, but the ducks were quacking idiotically across the water.

"So did you get laid?" she said.

"Come on. You know I don't sleep with clients."

"Really? I thought that was your main source of nookie."

"And fuck you."

"Fuck you back."

"Can we get on with this?"

"With what? What do you need me for?"

"Tell me I'm nuts to take the case."

"You already took the case."

"Well, I can untake it too."

"You always say there ain't no upside to working for crazy people."

"Unless they're rich."

"And I always say you're in the wrong line of work for that."

"So you think I should take a pass on this one?"

"You only ask me that so you can disagree with me."

"That's how I think things through."

"You could just argue with a Magic Eight Ball. I got stuff I could be doing."

"Like what?"

"I'll think of something."

"Anyway it's not the same."

"Tarot cards? Coin flips?"

"Not the same."

"Who did you argue with before me?"

"You know very well who."

"And how did that work out for you?"

"See, that's the difference. Your *friends* can't divorce you. Now seriously, what do you think about it?"

She picked up the photo and gave it another look. "I think Gray sounds like a first-class nutjob and I'd be surprised if there's any brother at all. He probably sent the picture to himself and forgot that he did it. Or pretends to forget."

"But who took it? Where did he get it?"

"Sports photographer. *Duh.* It probably ran in the paper or *Sports Illustrated*, he saw himself in it, got all excited and sent it to himself from wherever he was at the time, and when he sobered up didn't remember anything about it."

"Sent it by courier?"

"So he says."

"So he says the desk clerk said."

"The desk clerk was probably at the party getting wasted with him and doesn't remember it either. They're probably lovers. That's probably why he had to move out of the hotel. Loverboy probably asked him to put some pants on or something and broke his heart."

"Desk clerk was female."

"So *he* said."

"God, you're bitter."

She smirked. "Am I? I think I'm cute."

"The photo doesn't look exactly like Gray though. Different hairstyle, different way of cocking his head, different — I don't know — *look*. He didn't seem to think it was himself."

"He probably can't recognize himself in the mirror without consulting a field guide. He's a whack job. Take his money down to Barnes and Noble and buy him a copy of the *Audubon Guide to North American Whackjobs* and keep the change."

"You're in rare form this morning. Rough night?"

"And fuck you, McBee."

"Fuck you back. Your girlfriend kick you out of bed again?"

She murdered him with that look again. Then added: "I mean it, start by finding his shrink. I bet he's got a psychiatric record as thick as one of your Chinese novels."

"I bet *Red Chamber* is better reading."

"Is it about a whackjob too?"

"It's about the life and adventures of a stone that fell from heaven."

"How — never mind."

"Anyway, I'm not sure. I've interrogated my share of lunatics, and this guy doesn't fit the profile. Weird, yes. Eccentric, paranoid. But he's also smart and lucid and oriented. He didn't say anything that was obviously disconnected from reality."

"What was that about him going to die?"

"Well, we're all going to die."

"Are you also having premonitions?"

"OK, I'll give you that one. I should start by checking his story anyway. I don't have much else to go on. So you want to help?"

"Depends."

"On?"

"Do I have to meet him?"

"Meet him? He'll fire me if he ever finds out I talked to you about it."

"OK, I'm in. Where do we start?"

"Let's see if there's a game tonight."

CHAPTER 4

YOUTHFUL FOLLY

They fell into their routine, spent the next couple of hours working the wires. McBride focused on the brother: looked up adoption information and made a list of local sports photographers. Figuring that Gray would check on his usage of the loaner laptop, he made a point of using it for this work. Meanwhile Sylvia used McBride's beat-up old machine to check on Gray: name searches, credit records, NYC arrest records, newspaper archives. They worked sitting on opposite sides of McBride's tiny dining table against the window that looked through the porch toward the lake. Now and then they looked up to pour another cup of coffee from the pot between them.

The heavy weather lifted, leaving shallow pools across the backyard, draining tier by tier down to the lake.

The Bruins were playing at home that night and McBride bought tickets online, and after a couple of hours of heads-down labor they loaded their gear into the Office and headed out.

The Office was McBride's Jeep Cherokee. A banged-up, discolored eyesore with worn-out carpet, greasy windows, and a back floor piled with empty Doritos bags and slimy Dunkin' Donuts cups. But it had an indestructible engine that he paid a neighborhood mechanic to keep in perfect condition. He drove it like he was delivering bodies to hell and didn't much care what they looked like when they got there.

.   .   .

They were three hours early for the game, an hour earlier than the Garden opened doors, so they went to McGann's for a pre-game drink. They sat at the bar. Sylvia always wanted to sit at the bar. She wouldn't stay any place if there wasn't room at the bar. McBride wondered about that sometimes. Either she didn't want anyone, including McBride, to get the idea they might be on a date, or more likely she preferred to maximize her freedom of action. Which maybe amounted to the same thing.

The place was packed as usual before any event at the Garden. The bartop was slick with spilled beer.

She ordered a Sam Adams. He called for a pint of Guinness. They decided to share a plate of nachos.

"How drunk were you last night?" Sylvia said.

"Not very. Gray does make a helluva martini though. Ice-cold first-class gin, shaken not—"

"You're not pulling my leg, are you?"

"What?"

"Your man doesn't exist. No police record. Anywhere. Not here, not New York, city *or* state — or any state. No address that looked like a match. No birth record. No adoption record."

"Parents?"

"Nope. No death records for those names in Arizona. No property records. Rich people can't disappear that easy."

"What about—"

"Nothing. Nil. Nothing on the PI databases. No telephone, no driver's license, no registered vehicles, not even a boat. No credit report. No identifiable Facebook account, or Twitter or LinkedIn or

GooglePlus or Vine or Instagram or Flipboard or Flickr or Tumblr or WordPress or anydamnedotherthing. Nada. Nobody gets this gone by accident."

McBride shook his head woefully and took a long draught of the Guinness.

"OK," he said, wiping the foam off his lip with the back of his hand, "so he's somebody else passing himself off as Morris Gray with a fake passport."

"So why?"

"Exactly. If he wants to disappear, why hire a private dick to find—"

"To find what?" Sylvia turned up her free hand. The other was frozen onto her mug. "The prodigal brother?"

A waitress brought their food and they both tucked in. Nacho mountain afloat on beer river. Sylvia waved at the bartender for another round. She had no trouble getting his attention.

"Friend of yours?" McBride said, nodding in that direction.

"Never laid eyes on him."

"He's been laying some on you."

"Whatever, McBee."

The bartender started the second Guinness and brought her second Sam Adams over.

"You didn't smile that big bringing me a beer," McBride said.

"It's still settling," he said, like he'd misunderstood, and turned away again, eyes last.

"So how did you make out with the mythical brother?" Sylvia said.

"Worse! I don't even have a passport number to work with, or parents' names."

"So what's your plan now?"

McBride playacted giving the question serious contemplation, pulled on his chin, munched a couple more nachos. "First thing, pal," he said at last, "we're gonna enjoy the shit out of this hockey game that Gray is paying for. Second, we're gonna go ask around at the hotel. Third, we're gonna have a very serious discussion with our client."

"We?"

"You might have to wait in the bar for part three."

"Maybe you could take me home first."

"Play it by ear."

Sylvia was struck with a thought. "I know you're too noble to work strictly for hire, but has it occurred to you that you could make a nice bill off this whackjob?"

"String him along pretending to look for the prodigal while I collect a large every day?"

"Precisely."

"What about my professional ethics?"

"Aren't they still in Mexico?"

"Cute. You know you're a cute girl, Sylly."

"You know I can break your arm, *Christian*."

"Well, don't. I need it to pick up the check."

They finished the nachos, chugged the last of their second beers, denied the smiley bartender the pleasure of pouring Sylvia a third, left generous cash on the bar, and headed back to the Garden.

CHAPTER 5

WAITING

They still had to wait a bit before they could get in, but they passed the time chatting up the ticket takers, the security cops, and the scalpers. Everybody got the treatment: big smiles, Sylvia's best attempt at bedroom eyes, and the pretext — "Hey, how ya doin', gonna be a great game! Have you seen this guy around, friend of mine — *Sports Illustrated*, can you believe it? — He's a huge Bruins fan. — This my buddy, Jennifer. — We're supposed to meet him, he's got our tickets, but my fucking phone died…"

McBride knew one of the security cops from the force, a friendly, lazy, likable, corrupt old bastard everybody called Stogie, and McBride couldn't even remember his real name anymore. He talked to him for a while, sketched him a generally accurate version of the case, minus the weirder details.

After careful study Stogie regretted that he still couldn't make the photo, observed that it was a fucked-up case, and said, "Good luck with that one, Mickey B!"

Only cops ever called him that. After an infamous Charlestown snitch.

Once they got inside they started working the concessions, the ushers, the janitors, the guards… As it drew close to game time they went down to the rinkside photographers' hole and passed the picture around. The shooters all said they *wished* they'd taken that shot, but not a one of them remembered seeing it anywhere or had any idea who the fan in the background was.

"What about the two blonds?" McBride said. "They look pretty memorable."

"We're here to shoot the game, not ogle the fans."

They could see however that the pic was taken from the shooter's box or close to it because it was *absolutely* of the opposite corner of the rink from exactly their angle.

Sylvia asked if they thought it could be a fake.

"A fake what?"

"Say you had a picture of a guy like that, could you Photoshop him into the shot?"

"Maybe, but why?"

"I don't know. Cause he's your buddy or whatever, so he can get his face on the front page of the sports section."

"It'd be a pain in the ass. With the reflections the way they are on the glass. Hard to make that look right. We're shooters though, not Photoshop geeks."

"And you get fired for doing shit like that," added one of the others.

* * *

They got a couple more beers and found their seats and sat down to watch the game. The Bruins played like hell the first period and left the ice at zero to two. They started to get their skates under them in the second period but couldn't make up the Rangers' lead. They started the third period at one to three, but at the two-minute warning they snuck one in, then switched to six-man offense the last minute and Lucic thundered in the tying goal. With the fans screaming their minds out, they fought the overtime to a draw, and finally lost in a shoot-out. It was a hell of a game, McBride and Sylvia put away three beers apiece and a basket of pretzels, and yelled themselves hoarse. Now all they had to do was kill another two hours till 2:00 a.m. They decided to drown them in gin in the Bar at the Taj. The sports fan lives a life of waiting. Endurance pays dividends. Invest in fate. Sooner or later everyone's number comes up.

CHAPTER 6

CONFLICT

When the name of the hotel is the Taj, everything else in the place needs a generic name to offset it. The café is called the Café and the bar is called the Bar.

McBride stomped the Office to a halt in front of the place and jumped out leaving the door open. He trotted around to get the door for Sylvia but the valet beat him to it. McBride handed him a twenty and led a second twenty across the sidewalk to the doorman.

"Has Mr. Gray been down yet? Have you seen him today? He's my client. Told me to meet him here. I'm late as all hell but I haven't been able to reach him on the phone. Wondered if you guys had seen him go out?"

The doorman allowed that he knew him, but said he hadn't seen him for a couple of days.

"Hell, he didn't check out, did he?" McBride said, devastated.

The doorman — talking to McBride but looking at Sylvia — said, "No, he's still here. Mr. Gray don't go out much, but when he does it's always at 10:00 a.m. sharp."

"No kidding?" McBride said, while Sylvia rolled her head sadly. "He's a strange bird, that guy. Set your watch by him. Not that I have a watch. Keep breaking them!" He caught Sylvia possessively by the elbow. "Hey, thanks a bunch for your trouble, buddy."

"No trouble, sir," said the doorman, turning to watch Sylvia's backside swing away.

Inside the door Sylvia snarled, "You know, I'd like to—"

"Down weapons, pal. It's all for the cause."

There was a different manikin helming the desk tonight — red hair, green eyes, freckles, young, frog face — and they sauntered up and asked it if Mr. Gray, room eight-oh-eight, had come in yet.

"I haven't seen him," said the clerk. "I can ring the room if you like" — so bored he was aching to be helpful.

"No, that's OK," McBride said, "I'm meeting him in a little while anyway. I'll just check the bar first."

. . .

The place was an abyss, very empty and very dark, with blood red flourishes. They saddled two stools at the near end of the bar. The bartender was a short stout old man neatly dressed in the standard Taj costume, black slacks, white oxford shirt, and gold silk vest. He slid two napkins in front of them. McBride slid the photo back. Bartender was shaking his head before McBride asked him if he recognized the fellow in the picture.

"He lives here," McBride said. "Name's Morris Gray. Never comes in?"

Bartender didn't even glance at the picture. "If you know him, why are you asking me?"

"I just wondered if you knew him."

"What are you having?" End of discussion.

"How about a couple of martinis?"

"How about an ID?"

McBride's mood had begun to decline. "Are you serious?"

Bartender looked at him. In three seconds he was going to walk away. T-minus three…

McBride pulled out his driver's license and held it out for easy reading without handing it to him.

Bartender did not even glance at it. "Gin or vodka?"

"Not for me," Sylvia said. "I'm in the mood for champagne."

"That does sound good," McBride said. They ordered a bottle.

Bartender rolled away. He didn't ask Sylvia for ID.

"He's just grumpy because the Bruins lost," Sylvia said.

"Is that what we're celebrating, another ignominious defeat?"

"Tomorrow is another day."

"And tomorrow and tomorrow and tomorrow."

"Shakespeare again."

"Shakespeare had a lot to say about tomorrow. And all our yesterdays."

"Did he have anything to say about hockey?"

"More of a tennis fan, I think."

Bartender returned with the bottle and opened it and poured two glasses out. The hockey picture was still on the bar. He still didn't look at it.

"Speaking of yesterday," McBride said when he'd gone, "what *were* you up to last night when you should have been home in bed?"

"What makes you think I wasn't, Holmes?"

"You may have been in bed, but you weren't home in bed."

"Curiosity killed the cat."

"Trouble with — who are you dating now, Gladys Whatshername?"

"Yeah, no. Didn't work out."

"So?"

"So nothing. I had a bad day. Went to see Mom." (She was buried at St. Michaels.) "Drove around all night — half the night.

Out to Revere and walked down the beach. Slept in the car. Didn't want to go home."

"Oh. Is it her birthday already? Sorry I forgot."

"Tried to call Dad. I miss him so much."

"Why don't you go over for a visit for a while. Have you ever been?"

"We went once when I was nine."

"You could go for the holidays. See the Vatican. I hear it's nice. Pop in and say hi to the Pope. Give him my love."

CHAPTER 7

THE ARMY

Sylvia waited in the bar. McBride made a point of arriving at door number 808 four minutes early. First, he stood in front of it for a few seconds, in case Gray was peeping him. Then he put his ear against it, but heard nothing. Then he just waited, watching the clock on his phone, and the second it switched from 01:59 to 02:00, he knocked three times sharply.

Gray unlocked and unbolted the door five seconds later and pulled it open. He was dressed in scarlet silk pajamas.

McBride cracked up.

Gray looked puzzled. "What's funny?"

"What's funny? Just, you know, you look kind of naked without a stalk of celery in your pocket."

"What does that mean?" Gray said, without irritation. "You asked me not to appear in the nude and I obliged you."

"You, sir, are a gentleman," McBride said, "and a tomato," letting the door swing shut behind him.

"Lock the door, please, Mr. McBride. May I call you Christian?"

"No, you may not," McBride said, locking the door and throwing the bolt. "Nobody calls me that. But you can drop the 'mister' if you like."

"Just McBride. Would you like a martini, Just McBride?"

"*Judge* McBride." That was silly. Head buzzing. "Been looking forward to it all evening." How many drinks had he had tonight? Calculate. Two at McGann's, three at the game, half the bottle downstairs. That's two, five, seven or eight — several. He made an effort to appear sober. Dead giveaway, trying to look sober. "Have you made any improvements on your recipe today?" Fuck it.

"Not yet." Gray went to the bar and started mixing his bitch's brew. "What about you?"

McBride plucked the towel off the same chair as the previous night and plopped down. Dressed just for me. Sweet. "Me? I don't make 'em, just drink 'em." Was that a soft slur in his voice? Nothing anyone else would notice.

Still talking over his shoulder, Gray said, "I meant what about your progress? What do you have to report?"

"What do I have to report," McBride said, thinking out loud. "What do I have to report. Well, I did learn some things today, Mr. Gray." He put special emphasis on "mister."

"Already?" Gray sounded cheerful. He turned round smiling, shaking his mixer. He looked like a flaming statue of red Jell-O.

McBride cracked up again.

Gray waited for him to get control of himself, then observed, "Judge, I think you're drunk."

"And, *Gray*, I think you're full of shit."

Gray's face fell. His feelings were hurt. He turned away and poured the drinks without responding. Skewered two olives into each and brought them back. Just like old times.

"All right," Gray said, sitting down in the other chair. "What's on your mind?"

McBride took a sip of the martini. It was so good he wished he was sober enough to properly appreciate it.

"You don't exist, Morris Gray," he said, without taking out his notebook. "May I call you Morris Gray? Or is there some other made-up name you'd prefer tonight?"

"Morris will do," he said, quite seriously.

"Well, how about you tell me who you really are, and why you really hired me?"

"Tell me what makes you think I'm not who I say I am."

"Quit stalling."

"No, I really want to know. You saw my passport."

"I saw a document that looked like a passport. A beat-up seven-year-old passport without any entry stamps. How does a passport you never use get so worn? And if you don't travel, why is a passport the ID you have ready to hand in case someone inquires?"

"It's all I have."

McBride got his notebook out. "Driver's license?"

"I don't drive."

"Never?"

"I've never driven a car. Or a motorcycle."

"Boat?"

"Boat?"

"Social security card?"

"I don't need social security. I'm rich, and I don't have any income." Then with a resigned shrug, "Anyway, I won't live that long. When does it start now? At 70 years?"

"You never got a social security card?"

"I don't think so."

"School records?"

"I was tutored."

"College?"

"Never went. How about you? What was your concentration?"

Data point: not *major*. "Eight ball. With a minor in cheap beer."

"Eight ball?"

Data point. "Are you married?"

"Yes. — No."

"Divorced?"

"I'm not married."

"Never?"

"Not — no."

Data point: *hesitation*. "Gay?"

"For God's sake."

"Does the question offend you?"

"All your questions offend me, Judge."

"Ever been laid at all?"

"Laid?"

Data point. "When's the last time you left this room?"

"Two days ago."

"Who are you hiding from?"

Gray's eyes narrowed and his mouth set like he was pleased that McBride had finally asked the right question, but he didn't answer it.

McBride waited, glaring at him.

Finally Gray said, "Can't you guess?"

"Why are you hiding from him?"

Gray grew more impatient. He was an impatient man. "Do you like games of chance?"

"Hunh?"

"I suppose as a hard-nosed detective you like everything orderly and square and deterministic. I bet you're a chess player."

"What are you talking about?"

"Do you play cards? Bridge? What about poker?"

"Poker. Sometimes."

"Excellent! Let's play some cards!" Gray bounced up and went into the other room and returned with a square leather case. He sat down again and turned his chair toward the table between them and opened the case. It contained, nestled like miniature armies in velvet-lined pockets, two decks of cards, four dice, and several short stacks of poker chips. "I've been learning to play poker. But I don't have anyone to play with. Do people play five-card stud these days, or Texas hold 'em?"

"What people?"

"What's popular? What game do you like?"

"Hold 'em is pretty standard in casinos."

"Casinos. Right. And blackjack."

"Sure."

"Twenty-one." Practicing his erudition.

"I don't have time for this," McBride said.

"I'm not stalling. I'm just bored."

"Someone's waiting for me."

"Just a few turns."

Data point: *not "hands."*

"We can play while we talk." He started shuffling the cards awkwardly.

McBride sighed dramatically and took the deck away from him and started riffling it. "We'll be here till dawn the way you shuffle. Put your blind down. Keep talking."

Gray slid a $10 chip to the center of the battlefield. Drawing fire. "The day after I received the photograph, someone called me at the hotel."

"You told me no one called."

"I lied." He turned his palms up helplessly. He almost looked believable.

"Why?"

"I didn't think you would believe the real story."

McBride doubled the blind and dealt the pockets slowly. "Contrary to what you see in the movies, the real story is *always* more believable. What did your caller say?"

"He asked me if I had received the photograph. I asked him who he was. He said, 'Don't you recognize yourself?'"

McBride nodded at the cards. "Bet. And keep talking."

"I said, 'What do you want?' He said, 'Money, of course.' 'Money for what?' 'For your brother.' That was the first time in my life I'd ever heard that I had a brother."

"Well what did you think when you saw the photo?"

"I didn't know what to think. I guess I thought it was a joke."

"A joke?"

"I still don't believe my parents knew about him. I don't believe they would have kept it from me."

"Who would separate twins at birth?"

"I don't know. Is that so hard to believe in these times?"

"What's hard to believe is getting more relative by the minute. Bet."

Gray, smiling, slapped a $10 chip down like a cannon shot.

"Don't be an ass." McBride discarded the burn and dealt the flop. "How much money did he want?"

"One-hundred-thousand dollars."

"But you said no."

"I hung up."

"He never called back?"

"I left the hotel that night."

"What hotel?"

"I told you yesterday. The Essex."

"You told me five minutes ago you're a liar. Why didn't you call the police?"

"I'm willing to play along with your interrogation up to a point, McBride. But I draw the line at answering ridiculous questions."

"I'll make a note. What time did your man call?"

"Twenty-two-hundred."

Data point: *military time*. "What day?"

"December 27th."

"You've been in hiding ever since?"

"I've always been in hiding."

"But your caller knew you."

"He knew my face. His face."

"Is it a picture of him or of you?"

"It's not me."

"Then how did he know about you?"

"That's what you will find out."

"Your pair of jacks bets."

Gray's two princes surveyed the field. He reinforced them with another ten-spot.

McBride called and dealt the turn cards angrily, adding more rags to his worthless hand. "What's your real name?"

"I don't have a real name."

"What the fuck does that mean?"

"I told you. I've always been in hiding."

"Since you were born?"

"Moses was."

"Moses? Cut the crap and tell me your name."

"Which name?"

McBride slammed a matching chip down on the table, disturbing the troops.

Gray shook his head sadly, burdened with regret. "There's no name I can give you that will help you because I use different names all the time."

"The doorman knows your name, Morris. And the desk clerk knows your name, Morris. And I know your name, Morris. And the prodigal brother knows your name, Morris. And if you want me to find that brother, Morris, you're going to tell me the name he knew you by."

Gray frowned indulgently. "I hired you to find the name of the man in that picture. Knowing one or two of my names won't help you do that. None of my names matter. A rose by any other name would—"

"You're a horse's ass."

"Oh, that's a wonderful expression!" Gray giggled, and his scarlet silk pajama shirt shimmered disturbingly.

McBride dealt the river and snarled, "Bet."

Gray studied his cards, half a grin on his face.

Time passed.

More time passed.

McBride waited impatiently, unpleasantly drunk, feeling himself a fool for not walking out on this gig. But Gray had the hook in him now. He hated himself for that, and he hated Gray for knowing he had the hook in him.

At last the glaciers of analysis retreated and Gray merrily fielded yet another regiment of ten.

McBride flipped another bullet into the cauldron and said, more calmly now, "Why did you panic when he called? What kind of danger do you think you're in?"

Suddenly Gray looked as grim as an executioner. "The worst kind," he said, his voice a whisper. "You can't imagine. Worse than mortal."

His tone struck McBride. "Who are you protecting?" he said.

"People you can never know."

McBride tossed his hand. "I surrender."

CHAPTER 8

HOLDING TOGETHER

Sylvia was sitting in the lobby with her long legs stretched out in front of her. She looked sleepy.

"The bartender announced last call three seconds after you left," she said, getting up stiffly. "I had them fetch your car twenty minutes ago. I'll drive. Are you still employed or can I tell the fat doorman to kiss my sweet ass?"

"Not yet," McBride said, yawning. "Christ, I'm beat."

"You're beat? I've been up since five. Don't bring me on any more of these 2:00 a.m. rendezvous. How many more martinis did you have?"

"Two or three."

"I'll drive."

"We could just get a room."

"Maybe I *will* break your arm."

"We're coming back here in a few hours anyway."

"I'm not. I'm going home."

"Come on, Syl. I need you."

She turned on him like she was going to drop him.

"On the case!" he said defensively. "Would you calm the fuck down, please?"

They argued for a few minutes just inside the revolving door. Sylvia agreed — and promised justifiable homicide if he made a play for her.

He said he believed her and went outside to tell the valet to put the car back. He slipped him another twenty, saying, "It's Mr. Gray's money."

"Even better, sir," said the valet.

The room (double bed) was another $350 plus tax. McBride told the desk clerk to put it on Mr. Gray's bill.

"I'll have to get approval from Mr. Gray for that."

"Call him," McBride said. "He's up."

The clerk phoned up to Gray's room. Gray asked to speak to McBride.

"It's late. I'm drunk and I'm tired and it's a long way home and I have to come back to town tomorrow anyway to show your goddamn photo around and what do you care? You can afford it."

"Who are you with?" Gray said suspiciously.

"None of your business." Not strictly true, but McBride figured he didn't owe Gray more truth than he was getting from him. He handed the phone back to the clerk, saying, "Any floor except eight."

In the elevator on the way up, Sylvia said, "So, you didn't quit and you didn't get fired. Did you get any useful information?"

McBride slumped against the oak-paneled wall. "Story number one is beginning to unravel."

"So there's a story number two?"

"The brother is the one who sent the photo. And he called Gray the next day and offered to introduce himself to him for a hundred grand. And Gray's name isn't Gray."

"Well we knew that. What is his name?"

"He won't give it up."

"But you're still employed?"

"Yes."

The elevator stopped and they looked for their room. McBride was so fagged out he couldn't figure which way the door numbers went, left and right.

Sylvia led the way.

He followed, watching her heart-shaped ass swing like a metronome. He couldn't help himself. Besides, he was too drunk to do anything about it, even if she didn't tear all his limbs off, so what was the harm.

"I hope," she said, slipping the keycard into the door, "you're not going to all this trouble just to break it to me slowly that you have love for another man, McBee. Because you know I'm down with that. Especially if it's a kinky sugar daddy kind of thing."

"Aw, thanks, Syl. You're a real pal."

They went in. She hit the lights. It wasn't as big as Gray's room, but it was similarly appointed: thick bronze carpet, gold curtains and bedspreads, brocade chairs, maple desk.

"What a dump," she said. "Is this how your lover lives?"

"Only more so," he said.

"Poor slob." She flopped down on her back on the farther bed and blew a world-weary breath out through her lips.

He sat down on the other bed and started pulling off his shoes and socks.

"Well, are you buying the new-and-improved story?" she said.

"About a third. I buy that he's a paranoid S.O.B. And I buy that somebody scared him and scared him bad. And I might buy that the person who scared him is the man in the photo."

She looked over at him skeptically. "Really? You think you might buy this brother bullshit? You don't think it's just his own picture? Or a fake?"

"No. Why would we be here if it was a fake?"

"Because he's a lunatic. Because he's lonely and he can't sleep and he needs somebody to drink with at two in the morning and he's got the money to buy that company and he doesn't like hookers."

"And to keep me interested he's making up this silly mystery fable? Seems like quite a production. He could just go down to the bar and make bedroom eyes at the bartender."

"Come on, McBee, use your imagination. Maybe he has a thing for detectives. Maybe he likes mind games." She rolled onto her side toward him. "Maybe he's been going through the private detective listings alphabetically. You should ask around."

"Are you being serious?"

"Are you? Why are you playing along with his game? Even if a third of it is on the level, he's still two-thirds crazy as shit."

He pulled off his shirt and lay back on the bed to think about it. "If we stick with it," he said to the ceiling, "if we keep eliminating the alternatives, all these little rivers of bullshit will run together into the sea of truth."

"Poetic. Or maybe you're just trying to rationalize your participation in this farce."

"Maybe."

CHAPTER 9

THE TAMING POWER OF THE SMALL

He woke up later, still in the same position, flat on his back on the bed, and his feet on the floor completely numb. According to the red-faced clock on the table between the beds it was 5:09 a.m. Sylvia was asleep on her side, her back to him. She'd kicked the bedspread onto the floor and was covered by the sheet below the waist, but her back was bare. Neither of them had closed the curtains, and in the dim light from the street he could vaguely make out the shapes of the tattoos coiling over the olive skin of her back.

He'd seen them before, at the beach. On one of their double-date excursions they'd spent a weekend out on the Cape. The three women got along so well he'd started to wish they'd left him behind. One night, he got out of bed horny and unsatisfied and went down to drink a beer in the dark, and he heard Sylvia and her weekend girlfriend getting each other off upstairs. It made him so furious he went outside and stomped up and down the beach in his bare feet, threw his beer into the waves, and finally fell asleep on the sand. A month later, Hannah filed papers.

Her art was fascinating — flowers and vines and dragons — first-class work. He thought there was more there now than he'd seen at the beach, but it was too dark to be sure. Work in progress. It was all one of a kind work. She got her artistic friends to draw the designs. So far she didn't have any that showed outside of jeans and a t-shirt. Long tough muscles like a dancer or a boa constrictor.

One of their neighbors around the lake, Tony somebody, had expressed his appreciation for her looks one night over beers by calling McBride "one lucky bastard."

"I really don't think of her that way," McBride said, feeling sour.

"Yeah, right. You don't even notice what a hard little ass she has."

"I notice. But I don't dwell on it. It'd fuck up our relationship if I did."

Tony didn't get invited to the next party.

McBride pulled his dead legs onto the bed, took off his pants, and got under the covers. But he didn't sleep well. Daylight was coming on already. He was too beat to get up and draw the curtains, and he didn't want Sylvia to catch him walking around her side of the room in his skivvies. He lay there a long while listening to the whisper of her breath and watching the shadows on the ceiling waver and shift as the traffic passed by below.

CHAPTER 10

TREADING

McBride drifted in and out until a knock on the door woke him up completely. He glanced at the clock. Nearly 9:00. He rolled out of bed and went to the door in his shorts and opened it without peeping first, expecting to see a maid.

There stood Gray smiling like he'd just hit the lottery and dressed to the nines — tailored pin-striped blue silk suit that looked like it had just been buffed and polished, a maroon damask silk vest, a flaming orange shirt, a paisley silver necktie, and real blue suede shoes.

McBride was struck dumb.

Gray rose on his toes and scanned the room over McBride's shoulder. "I thought I'd treat you and Sylvia to breakfast. The baked salmon benedict is excellent."

McBride could not have been more stunned if the archangel Gabriel had just told him he was with child. He heard Sylvia rustling in the sheets behind him.

"Invite me in, McBride," Gray said. "Introduce me to your—" He hesitated, losing track of his noun.

"What the fuck, Morris."

"You know," Gray teased, "you only call me that when you're angry." Oh, they were best buddies.

"What the fuck, Morris," McBride said again. He couldn't get his mind any further down the road than that.

"Stand aside, my man!" Gray said grandly, waving him back.

McBride gave way and Gray stepped through.

Sylvia sat up blinking in the middle of the bed, letting the sheet fall to her waist, as Gray emerged from the vestibule trailed by McBride. The room was now flooded with morning light and Sylvia's colorful tattoos danced and shone on her stomach and chest.

McBride wanted to tell her to cover the hell up, but his jaw had fallen on the carpet.

"Well, hello there!" Gray beamed, like a politician accosting a pile of cash. "Good morning! I'm Morris Gray, Mr. McBride's current employer." Treading over McBride's mandible, he crossed the room quickly to Sylvia's side and thrust out his hand. "I'm delighted to meet you, Miss Sylvia. I'm sorry, I don't know your last name."

"Hi," she said, taking his hand while running the fingers of her other hand through her bed hair.

"You're the most beautiful thing I've seen in a month," Gray said, without releasing her hand. In fact, he clapped his left on top of it while he frankly scanned her up and down. "You look like, I don't know, a tiger in a jungle. Tyger, tyger, burning bright."

McBride wasn't sure but he had the impression that Sylvia was flattered.

Her left nipple was the focus of an elaborate blue and green mandala. Her right breast sported a pink chrysanthemum bloom. There was nothing tiger-like on her.

"Why don't you both get dressed," Gray said, looking only at Sylvia, "and come down to breakfast in the Café?"

She smiled. "Sure."

"Then I'll go ahead and have the coffee ready." He nodded in McBride's direction: "Our friend looks like he could use it." There was a twinkle in his eye when he said it.

McBride grimaced painfully. Should have brought the gun.

Gray made his departure.

McBride stood gaping and frowning furiously at Sylvia.

"So that's him," she said, pulling the bedsheet over her breasts at last. "Not quite what I expected."

McBride took control of his thoughts with a will and remarked in a cold voice: "I see you have some new ink."

Sylvia looked away and swung her legs off the far side of the bed. "I need a shower."

"I need a fire hose."

She shot a look back at him, but he ducked into the bathroom.

CHAPTER 11

PEACE

The maitre d' in the Café greeted them like friends and said before they opened their mouths, "Mr. Gray is already seated. Follow me, please."

Gray had a corner booth big enough for six people by the window. The light of heaven smashed through the big glass behind him, illumining him like he was dressed in neon. Morning had broken, like the first spring. Christ descending in power and tailored silk. He'd shed his jacket somewhere, revealing more of the fire-orange shirt: the delicately damasked maroon vest only just managed to contain the eruption.

McBride tossed his lumpy fishing jacket on one of the spare chairs and slid into the booth on Gray's right. Three places were set, or rather three of the six that fit the table had been removed. Gray had claimed the middle one. Sylvia slid in on the other side.

The waiter had followed them to the table and before they were settled he was filling their cups with coffee from the pot on the table. He topped off Gray's cup too.

Gray dumped a couple of heaping teaspoons of sugar in after it and a generous slug of cream, gave it a vigorous stir, and raised a toast.

"Cheers!" His mood was as bright as his costume. When McBride and Sylvia didn't respond right away, neither having ever toasted with coffee, Gray added — in an accent that was not his, nor anyone else's — "Top of the mornin' to ya," (ducking his cup toward Sylvia, then McBride) "ladies and germs!"

Sylvia laughed.

McBride's head was ringing.

"They have free newspapers if you'd like one," Gray said pleasantly.

"How do you know her name?" McBride said.

Gray was briefly startled, then: "You told me last night."

"The hell I did."

"Yes, you told me you didn't have time to play cards because you had a date."

"You were playing cards!" Sylvia said.

"I didn't say I had a date," McBride said, "I said—"

"You were drunk," Gray said. "You don't know what you remember." He turned to Sylvia. "Yes, we played two hands of Texas hold em'. It was my idea. I sincerely apologize for keeping you waiting. Next time, of course, you'll join us. Do you play cards?"

"You were playing cards!" she said again.

"I didn't say I had a date," McBride repeated to Gray, "I said—"

"What is your last name, by the way?" Gray said to Sylvia, ignoring him.

"Conti."

"Conti. Right." He regretted having forgotten.

Data point. Who was making notes on who?

The waiter returned already. The place was busy but he didn't seem to have anyone else to wait on. "You'll have the usual, Mr. Gray?" he said. "Yes? — And what about the lady?"

"I recommend the salmon benedict," Gray said.

Sylvia acquiesced — a mere formality, as the waiter had already moved on to McBride.

"I'll have the same," he mumbled, and gulped down half his cup of coffee, black.

The waiter glided off through the crowded tables like a goldfish through a frog pond.

Gray turned his back on McBride and stretched an orange-sleeved arm casually onto the bench back behind Sylvia. "Now then, what do you do? Tell me about yourself."

She noticed the arm, and smiled, and didn't withdraw, and said, "I do what I like mostly."

"And what do you like?"

McBride stood an elbow on the table to hold his face up while he listened.

"I garden. I work out. I hang with friends. I read a lot."

"Do you neither toil nor spin?"

"I help McBee with his cases from time to time," — she smiled across the table at her sometime partner — "if he asks me nicely."

McBride grinned sarcastically with half his mouth.

"And does he pay you for these services?" Gray said.

"If she asks me nicely."

"You have money then?" Gray continued with her.

"I live cheap," she said. "I do legal research now and then when I'm in the mood."

"Do you — I don't know what word to use — *copulate* with Mr. McBride?"

She hit him hard with a look.

McBride wagged his head low over his coffee.

"I'm just curious," Gray said.

"Curious is not the word that occurred to me," Sylvia said.

Gray lit up with a big smile. "Perhaps I'm rude to ask. But I can't be bothered to care about such things. I'm interested in you." He turned his head slightly in McBride's direction and tacked on, "In both of you."

"We're just friends," McBride mumbled.

"Good friends?" Gray said, still looking at Sylvia, studying her brassy eyes.

"Just good friends," she said, cool, but soft.

"What did you have planned this morning?" Gray said, as if to hear their excuse for spending the night together in a room he had paid for.

McBride answered to the back of Gray's head: "It's like this, Morris. I was going to hit the bricks and continue trying to find somebody who could make that photo you gave me. Meanwhile Sylvia here was going to hang out in the park across the street and try to spot you leaving, then tail you wherever you went."

Sylvia raised him a questioning look.

"Tail?" Gray said, looking back and forth between them.

"Follow."

"Follow me? Shadow. Why?"

New word. Data point: who doesn't know what a tail is?

"Because the new-and-improved version of your story is as full of holes as the original. I'm not likely to find your long-lost brother until I know who you really are and what your game is. So if you won't tell me, I'm going to have to find out the hard way."

The waiter arrived with breakfast during this speech and dealt their identical three plates with quiet efficiency.

"There's really nothing to find out," Gray said as the waiter refreshed their coffees. "I mean really, nothing. It's no use to *tail* me. As I said last night, it won't help you."

"I'll decide what I find helpful."

"But it's my party."

"Come again?"

"I'm paying you to do what I tell you to do."

Oh the humanity. "How many detectives did you hire before me?" McBride said. "Or try to hire?"

"None."

"You're paying me to find somebody. If you think you know how to do that better than me, do it yourself."

"There are reasons why that's not practical."

"Because you're paranoid? For a man who's supposed to be hiding you've certainly been making a spectacle of yourself. Most expensive hotel in town. Everyone in the joint at your beck and call. Dressing like a three-alarm fire."

Gray grinned at that, flattered. "I'm just the fanciest fish in a very small aquarium. It's all I have now. Just a little more time in this little world. I want to make the most of it. Is that so wrong?"

"If you went into hiding because you were afraid of the brother, why are you trying to find him now?"

"Because I want to know, as you say, what his *game* is."

"That's cute, but it's not an answer. You're too clever by half."

"It is my tragic flaw," Gray said, enlarging his morning smile again, and training it back on Sylvia.

"Mine too," she said, smiling back. "We should start a support group. The Too Clever By Half Club."

McBride clattered his coffee extra loud.

"But seriously," she added. "Why *are* you trying to find him?"

Nice of her to show up for work.

"Your McBride asked me last night, though he probably doesn't remember it, who I was protecting." Gray studied the ceiling for a moment, but decided the answer wasn't there. "No, I have good reasons. Probably, however, I will never be able to share them with you."

"That's a shame." She sounded regretful.

Sincerely regretful. McBride stabbed the tablecloth with his coffee spoon.

"You're welcome to spend the day with me," Gray said to her. "Wouldn't that be much more pleasant? I'll enjoy the company.

Besides, it's too late to *tail* me now that your partner has" — he searched a moment for the right cliché — "let the cat out of the bag."

"And what's on for today?"

"I have an errand to run this morning, and then I'm going to play it by ear."

CHAPTER 12

STANDSTILL

McBride called her from behind the wheel of the Office at 4:30. "There's another game on at the Garden tonight," he said. "Where are you?"

"Oh, hello," she answered. She sounded surprised to hear from him. "We're just having tea and scones in the French Room. Do I have to go to the game?"

"Yes. I'll pick you up."

"What time?"

"Twenty minutes. Tear yourself away."

"*Jawohl, mein Kapitän.*"

He could hear her saluting.

. . .

He double-parked in front of the Taj and called her from the curb. It took her ten minutes to come down. He was about to call her back when she appeared, stepping out through the rotating doors like a cat parading on a fence rail.

"Payback is it?" McBride said as she got in.

"What?"

"For keeping you waiting last night." He threw the Office into gear and yanked it into traffic more abruptly than he'd planned. There was a long angry honk from behind.

"Oh, I'm over it," she said, nonchalant.

"Have you been here all day?"

"No. We went out after breakfast."

"At 10:00 o'clock?"

"Yes."

"On the dot?"

"I think so."

"Where?"

"We walked through the Garden and rented a rowboat. You know, he really he is like a child. You'd think he'd never seen such wonderful things before."

"A real babe in the woods."

"He couldn't stop looking at all the squirrels and geese and dogs. We saw a man with a pet monkey. Morris asked me if I thought it was a 'real' monkey."

"What else?"

"That's what *I* said."

"What else did you do?"

"Oh. We went shopping. He bought me a new blouse. Do you like it?"

He hadn't even noticed. Some detective. He looked over at her now. It was green and shimmery and expensive. "Very nice," he said, not meaning it, though it was true. "What else?"

"Well, we went to the bank."

"Ah!"

"What?"

"He has a bank account!"

"Rich people do that."

"But he has one in town. What did he do there?"

"Visited his safe-deposit box."

"Did you go in with him?"

"No."

"Why the hell not?"

"He told me to wait."

"Well, hell, Sylvia."

"I know. Life sucks."

"Did he say anything about why he needed to visit his safe-deposit box?"

"Yes, he said he needed money."

"He keeps it in a box?"

"Apparently."

"How much did he get?"

"I don't know. A lot."

"How much of a lot?"

"I saw it later, when we got back to the hotel. He had it tucked away in various pockets."

"You went back to his room with him?" He almost succeeded in keeping the surprise out of his voice. Or was it scorn?

She looked over at him, but he didn't look back.

"What size bills?" he said. "Were they loose or wrapped?"

"Wrapped. Hundreds, I suppose."

"How many bundles?"

"Two or three."

"Well, which, two or three?"

"Five."

"He got out fifty grand?"

"If you say so."

"What bank?"

"Sovereign."

"Two blocks away. Then what?"

"We had lunch at Nine Park."

"Across the Garden. So you just walked everywhere?"

"Yes. It was just a beautiful day. Actually I had a lovely time. What did you do today?"

"Then back to the Taj?"

"We sat on a bench by a mulberry tree in the Garden for a while. There was a family trying to fly a kite. But there wasn't much wind. It kept sinking back. The little boy cried."

"Aw. Bad kite day. What else?"

"Morris read poetry."

McBride nearly rear-ended the car ahead of him. "He what?"

"He read poetry."

"Out loud to you?"

"Yes. It was charming."

"What kind of poetry?"

"Nature poetry."

"From a book?"

"Yes, from a book. We stopped at the Barnes & Noble by Emerson and he bought a little book of twenty-first century nature poetry."

"You left that out."

"Oh no!" She clapped her hands to her cheeks. Edvard Munch. "Will my punishment be very, very severe?"

McBride started to respond but stopped himself just in time.

"It was called *The Sky Is Higher Than You Think, The Earth Is Lower Than You Know*. Morris thought that was a very funny title."

After a moment he said, "So how was my day?"

"So how *was* your day?"

"Swell. I shopped that damn photo around to every photographer I could catch. I even paid a visit to my old unit and got them to run a face-recognition search on it."

"Anything?"

"Not a damn thing. And now I owe Willy Cook a favor. And I can't stand that S.O.B."

"Well, he probably feels the same about you, right?"

"We're getting nowhere."

"Perseverance."

"Want to get some eats before we head over to the Garden?"

CHAPTER 13

FELLOWSHIP WITH MEN

They parked the Office and walked to McGann's and sat in the same seats they'd had the night before — at the bar.

"So what's the deal with always sitting at the bar?" McBride said.

"I like to sit at the bar."

"I bet you don't make your man Morris sit at the bar."

Sylvia swung her head around like she was aiming a cannon. "My god, McBee, you're jealous." A look of amused alarm widened her face.

He glared at her, eye to eye, and her eyes in the barlight were like two emerald flames.

Three hours to game time but the place was already getting busy. Two shirts in three were black and gold Bruins jerseys. Happy sounds of fellowship and team spirit.

The same bartender was on duty. Just like old times. McBride ordered a black and tan. Sylvia ordered a vodka martini, dirty, on the rocks. Three kinds of sacrilege.

"You hate martinis," McBride said.

"Since when?"

"Did Gray make you a martini?"

"Yes. It was excellent."

Damned for all time.

"No, I'm not jealous really," McBride said. "I've just had a shit day. I was hungover all morning, and I'm sick of flagging that damn picture all over town, and I'm really sick of playing this fuckwit's game."

"So quit."

"So you walked everywhere today, no taxis?"

"That is correct," she said with acute precision and a sharp little nod.

"And all just around the Garden and the Common?"

In the same tone: "Also correct."

McBride ignored her taunting and stared at the television behind the bar and mulled. The luminaries on ESPN anticipated another Rangers win. Somebody yelled, "Fuck ESPN!" Somebody else, "Fuck the Rangers!" A cheer went up. Barbarians at the gate, united in defiance.

The bartender returned with Sylvia's indecent martini — he also left a black and tan for McBride since he happened to be in the same neighborhood.

"I never told Gray your name," McBride said.

"What?"

"Last night. I never told him your name. But he called you by name when he came to our room this morning. How did he know your name?"

"Maybe he got it out of the desk clerk. He paid for the room after all."

"I never told the desk clerk your name either. Did you?"

"Why would I?"

"So how did Morris know your name? Maybe he already knew you."

"He only knew my first name. Knew me how?"

"You two certainly got along well."

"He's a charming man. Weird. But charming."

"You certainly seemed comfortable showing him your tits."

Sylvia let her martini glass come down hard on the bartop. "What is your deal, McBee?"

First he scowled, then thought better of it and hung his head, playacting shame. "I'm sorry. It's just — Something about this guy just throws me off my game."

"Well, get over yourself. He's a client. It's a paycheck. Do the job."

McBride stared up at the luminaries for a while, quietly smoldering. He had to admit to himself that he was pissed not because she had scolded him but because she was right.

"You know, it's not because he's lying about something," he said in an even tone after a few smoldering minutes of cogitation. "That goes with the territory. And it's not because I don't know what he's lying about, because as far as I can tell he's lying about pretty much everything. The thing that is bugging the shit out of me is that I can't figure what he's lying about exactly. He's not lying for the usual reason, to protect himself. He's said a couple of times that he's protecting someone. And that's the one thing he said that felt like it came from the heart."

Sylvia nodded her head. "But you planted that idea, didn't you? Didn't he say you asked him who he was protecting?"

"Yeah, that's right. Christ, I was drunk. But I remember what he answered. 'People you can never know.' And he looked grim when he said it. Like a man with a price on his head and a mugshot on every lamppost."

"And now his picture *is* all over town."

"Well, I haven't given out any copies."

"And what's with the 'I'm gonna die soon' bit?"

"Did he talk about that today?"

"No."

"Did you get anything out of him, or was it all poetry in the park?"

"I was enjoying myself. I do that sometimes. You should try it."

"And you tell me to do the job."

The bartender came by again and offered them menus. McBride waved him off.

"I've been eating fancy food all day," Sylvia said. "I'm really looking forward to getting some fat pretzels and weak beer at the game."

"I'm going down to New York tomorrow," McBride said. "See what I can dig up on our man."

"Which one?"

"Either one. Want to come along? We could stay in town again tonight and head out early."

Sylvia looked doubtful. "I don't know. When's the last time I was home? Was it just yesterday morning? Feels like a week ago. Don't you want to change your shorts?"

"We'll buy new underwear. Expenses."

CHAPTER 14

POSSESSION IN GREAT MEASURE

They worked the arena that night the same as the night before, showed the photo to everyone they could catch, from scalpers to vendors to photographers. And they came up just as empty-handed.

One of the photographers took a picture of McBride's picture and offered to show it around back at the office. McBride told him there was $1000 waiting for the person who ID'd the subject.

Fortune smiled upon the home team. The Bruins vindicated last night's near miss by taking the Rangers back to hockey school. Tuukka Rask modestly manned the net with unfailing precision while the five sticks swarmed without embarrassment or mistakes around him. The Rangers were shut out four – zip and the Bruins headed to New York with the series even at 1 – 1.

McBride decided to skip the 2:00 a.m. meet up, took Sylvia home after the game, crashed in his own bed for a few hours, and set out after the Bruins at dawn, in clean underwear, to New York.

CHAPTER 15

MODESTY

McBride drove as far as the Bronx then took the subway into Manhattan and walked straight from 59th and Lexington to the Essex House with its head in the clouds. It was still morning, but a hundred-dollar tip got him a room. He asked about breakfast and was directed to the South Gate Tavern, which turned out to be a quaint name for the sparkling mirrored-glass and Italian-marble salon off the lobby where there happened to be food service. He showed his waiter Gray's photo, asked if he knew him, and got a believable "no." He asked the maitre d' with the same result. Likewise, after breakfast, the doorman, the desk clerk, and the concierge. He asked to speak with the hotel manager privately.

McBride handed his credentials and the photo across the manager's desk and explained he was on a case for a long-term guest of theirs, "Mr. Morris Gray."

The manager, a balding brown suit with an orange tie and matching pocket handkerchief, dropped his milky smile by half and said from behind his desk, "You understand we cannot provide any information about our guests."

McBride smiled a smile most guileless and most pure, altogether radiant with celestial light. "Oh, it's not *that*, you see. I already *know* the guest. He's my client! What I'm after is the fellow who delivered that photo. It's his *twin* brother." Gesticulating helpfully: "Mr. *Gray* hired *me* to find *him*. They haven't *seen* each other in, well, *ever*."

The manager's smile fell the other half. "Nevertheless. Unless it's a police matter—"

"Certainly! Certainly!" McBride dialed the warmth another notch yet. "I was a cop for 20 *years*! You don't need to tell *me*. I could tell you *stories*… Well, you can imagine! Actually, the thing is, it would be a big help to me if you could just verify a date. The date when that photograph was delivered for Mr. Gray. It would have been some time in December." As he spoke he checked his notes for effect. What he really wanted was confirmation that Gray had ever stayed here.

"I'm sorry," the manager said, "but I can't help you." He was Gibraltar.

They danced around like this for a few more minutes. The manager became impatient. McBride feinted and circled and humbled himself.

"Oh boy," McBride said, conjuring embarrassment, "I wonder if I've got the wrong place entirely! This *is* the Marriott Essex, right? Mr. Gray *did* check out of here toward the end of December, right? I mean *that* fellow, right?" He pointed at the photo.

Gibraltar gave the picture a final perfunctory glance, observing, "But you said this was the brother."

"Yes, sir, I did! Very good! But they're identical twins, you see!" McBride imagined he was killing him with bonhomie. Or at least critically injuring. "I just thought, you know, you might remember the face, if not the name. Gray is a forgettable name."

"No, I've never seen him." He offered the photo back over his desk as though he were offering the blessings of heaven. "Is there anything else I can do for you?" And the small rain down can rain.

Eat shit and die? "No. No. Thanks a bunch." The grin he pulled his face into nearly split his head off. "Sorry to take up so much of your time."

"Not at all," the manager said, getting up. "I am sorry I couldn't be more help, Mr. McBride. And welcome to the Essex."

CHAPTER 16

ENTHUSIASM

He asked the desk clerk and the maitre d' and the doorman what time they each got off work and the next shift came on, then to kill time he went outside, crossed 59th Street, and strolled into Central Park. It was the first really warm, bright day of the year, and the park was crawling with movement: small women running large dogs, two kids on long skateboards hanging off the back of a rickshaw, an endless swarm of competitive cyclists hurtling around the drive while minders yelled at mere pedestrians to watch out for their lives, college boys in T-shirts and backwards baseball caps sauntering along beside women in bright blazers and shorts so short they didn't show below the jacket.

He ambled through to Sheep Meadow and lay his body down on a receptive mound of grass in the shade of a great beech with a canopy like a thunderhead. He watched a yoga class twisting and bending in the sun.

He called Sylvia to see if she was making any progress on her end but she didn't answer.

He knew a detective named Ollie Garretson with the city's finest. New York and Boston were like complimentary poles of the northeast crime magnet. He and Garretson traded favors from time to time running down subjects at either end of the bar. You only used official channels when you didn't actually want to get anything done. McBride called him up and told him his tale of woe.

"Computer says there's nobody by that name in our fair city," Garreston said. "You got an alias maybe?"

"Just Morris Gray," McBride said. "I figure that's the alias." McBride gave Garretson the number off Gray's passport.

"No sosh?"

"No sosh. Anything you can cross it with?"

"Hang on."

Garretson fancied himself a dancer and a ladies' man. So they used to go to clubs where McBride could sit at the bar and watch him give the ex a twirl. Actually they were pretty good.

Garreston came back with the news. "Nada, McBird." Yes, there was no end to McBride's cute names. "Return to sender. No such number. No such zone." The joke around City Hall for a while had been that McDonald's was going to name a new sandwich after him: the McBastard. All bread and special sauce, no meat. "New York never heard of the cocksucker. So how's that lovely wife of yours doing these days?"

"She's great. We split a couple of years ago." It was four years actually, but that would make it seem like he hadn't kept in touch.

"Oh, yeah?" Garretson said. Was that opportunity knocking? "She still up in Beantown?"

"Not your type, Ollie."

"Or yours, I guess."

"It's all relative. Anyway, thanks for running that name for me. How about I buy you a drink later? You know that pub in Kips Bay we hit a few times?"

"I might be able to make that work."

McBride said he'd be there regardless and if Garretson could get away, all the better. But he figured Garretson wouldn't show if the ex wasn't along.

He had the Plotinus in his jacket pocket. There was always a book in his pocket. He took it out and tried to read over the distractions of the day. Evil actions must not be blamed on the universe. There is special providence in the fall of a sparrow. His attention wandered to the twisting yoga class. There were five women to every man. Colorful tights and mats. Like Easter eggs rolling on the lawn. Seeking reunion with God in the ground.

He dropped his book and lay back on the grass and stared up at the beech leaves spread over him and made an effort to apply his thoughts to the puzzle that was Morris Gray. This was a ludicrous kind of a job. But it was better than unemployment. Better still than wages.

The sun was warm and the breeze in the leaves was hypnotic.

Why didn't Sylvia answer his call? What was she up to now? He thought about her sitting up in bed with her tattoos bare. Thinking about her made him uncomfortable with himself. But his thoughts kept coming back to her the way your tongue keeps poking at a canker to see if it still hurts.

His phone buzzed in his shirt pocket, startling him. He fumbled getting it out and looked at the ID. Think of the devil.

He tapped and answered: "What's up, Syl?"

"It's me." A man's voice.

"It's me who — Morris?"

"Yes. Where are you?"

"I'm working your case. Where's Sylvia?"

"Are you in New York?"

"Yes."

"Why?"

"*I'm working the case*, Morris. I assume Sylvia is with you since you're on her phone?"

"There's nothing in New York."

"How do you know?"

"You're wasting your time, McBride."

"How about you don't tell me how to be a detective and I won't tell you how to be a lunatic. Deal? Let me talk to Sylvia."

"She's in the bathroom."

"Is lying just a bad habit with you or is it a principled thing?"

"Just a moment."

Noise of shuffling and muttering.

Sylvia came on: "I missed your call earlier. I was in the shower."

"Is that where you found Morris?"

"Honestly, McBee, I wish—"

"I take it the surveillance is going well?"

"Super. Is that what you called to ask?"

"Why can't he use one of his own damn phones to call me?"

"Ask him."

"I think it's because he wanted to make sure I knew he was with you. Did you go back to the city just to see him?"

"No, he's here."

"At your place?"

"Yes."

"He's at your place?"

"Yes."

"You're not at the Taj?"

"*No.* What's the problem?"

"Morris Gray is in your place. It's fucking creepy."

"No it isn't. Why is it?"

"Oh come on."

"Oh come on what?"

"Is he right there with you? What room are you in?"

"Jesus Christ."

"You're really bringing him out of his shell, Syl. What a man won't do to get a nice piece of ass, right?"

A beat passed while, he supposed, she was trying to compose herself.

"Speaking of ass," she said, "goodbye."

CHAPTER 17

FOLLOWING

Around 2:00 o'clock McBride roused himself from the grass and carried Plotinus back into the Essex for a late lunch and to interrogate the oncoming restaurant staff. He sat at the bar. Baked scrod that appeared to have been dropped in a pine forest on the way to the plate. But it was good. The intel was not.

The bartender was a friendly young woman, an aspiring composer, and a former Bostonian suffering divided sports loyalties. She'd studied at Berklee and now was finding her future in the Big Apple. They talked smack about the playoffs.

After lunch he ordered a martini. Not too dry. The olives came swizzled on a sliver of bamboo curled and tied on one end to make a handle — the same way Gray did it.

"Where'd you get the idea to skewer your olives like that?"

"That's just how they do it here."

"Where do you get the bamboo?"

"We buy them by the box."

"Already tied on the end?"

"Yup."

"Do you suppose there's an army of children in a jungle somewhere tying knots in bamboo swizzles for two bucks a day?"

"No. I suppose there's a machine that does it for free."

She asked him why he was looking for the man in the hockey photo. He invented a fable about the pair of women with him being wanted for questioning in connection with a human trafficking case. A good pretext should appeal to the sympathies of the mark. Most people enjoy telling you anything they think nobody else could. Your job is to help them feel this would be a virtuous act.

He asked her what kind of music she composed.

She said, "Avant-garde soundscapes."

"Interesting. What station do they play that on?"

"Strictly underground. My new piece is called 'Space Music from Hell.'"

"Really? Could you hum a few bars? Maybe I know it."

She smiled indulgently and hummed a few notes in 4/4 time: "Doo doodoo doo doo, doodoo doo doo…"

"I've heard that before. What are the lyrics?"

"*There's a lake of gin we can both jump in—*"

"Big Rock Candy Mountain! You didn't write that! I think you're pulling my leg."

"Sucks, doesn't it?"

"Touché." He tipped his drink to her.

She offered him another and he took it.

"You know that's really a filthy song," she said.

"It's about drugs, right?"

"No. It's a hobo trying to seduce a boy with promises of hobo paradise to become his punk. Nineteenth Century American Folk Music."

"You're shitting me."

"Scout's honor." She asked him about his book.

"Plotinus? Neoplatonian crusader against the gnostic hordes. He had a few things to say about music himself."

"Music of the spheres? Pythagoras? Like that?"

"The world is made of music. It harmonizes. Which isn't that far-fetched maybe."

She took it and opened to the page he had dogeared and read:

"All things and events are foreshown and brought into being by causes; but the causation is of two Kinds; there are results originating from the Soul and results due to other causes, those of the environment.

Nature vs. Nurture."

"And the problem of evil. Karma, free will, and guilt."

"What about music?"

He took it from her and flipped through a few pages and handed it back.

She read:

"Now in the case of music, tones high and low are the product of Reason-Principles which, by the fact that they are Principles of harmony, meet in the unit of Harmony, the absolute Harmony, a more comprehensive Principle, greater than they and including them as its parts.

See, I get that. That makes sense to me."

McBride noticed, as she held the book, tattoos on the backs of both hands, a treble clef on the right, bass clef on the left. What the fuck was Morris Gray doing at Sylvia's house? Having a second look at her tats?

CHAPTER 18

WORK ON WHAT HAS BEEN SPOILED

Later he went back to his room, showered, changed his clothes, and headed back out. The doorman flagged him a taxi. Twenty bucks later he stepped out on the sidewalk in front of Paddy Reilly's and went inside. He looked around but, as expected, he didn't see Garretson.

The band, a duo, was just sitting down to play. An accordion player of all things. And a drummer with a variety of bells, blocks, and hand drums spread about, including, of course, a bodhrán. They called themselves "Föhn."

McBride settled down at the bar and called for a pint and a menu. He couldn't remember the last time he'd been here. Years.

Föhn turned out to be pretty good. They could shag a fast jig with hair-raising energy, and on the slow numbers the accordionist could wail like a lovelorn banshee.

McBride noticed a woman standing near the bar, tapping her heels and drinking a pint — white, five-five, one-thirty-five or -forty, approximately forty years old, pie-faced and freckled, long fine wavy blond hair, square shoulders and strong arms like a farmer, faded blue denim shirt, blue jeans, and cowboy boots that weren't shiny. He saw that she noticed him looking at her. The band finished their first set, and she tossed down the last of her pint, turned and gave him a look, made up her mind, and stepped over to the bar next to him.

"How about I buy you a drink, cowboy?" she said, drawing a crooked smile to her thin lips. "Unless you're old-fashioned."

"What if I am?"

"Then you can buy *me* a drink. My name is Cora."

"That's an old-fashioned name."

"Yeah, well, I didn't pick it."

"McBride."

"Sure that's not your first name."

"Nobody calls me by my first name. What's your other name?"

"Lobb. Cora Lobb. Licensed to kill."

"Thanks for the warning."

Leaning over the bar she caught the eye of one of the bartenders and showed him two fingers. He nodded and added two more glasses to the queue at the Guinness tap. She turned around and leaned back against the bar with her elbows on the rail. Her pose gave her chest a distracting effect.

"So what brings you to town, last name McBride?"

"How do you know I'm not local?"

"I can tell."

"I'm working a case." He could have said just "business" or "work," but "a case" invited another question.

She asked it: "A case? You a lawyer or something?"

"Private investigator."

She lowered her chin and looked up at him skeptically. "Really?"

"Cross my heart and hope to die."

"What a fucked-up expression, 'hope to die.'"

"Hope to die if it's a lie."

"I don't hope to die for any reason. I think dying is highly overrated. What are you private investigating?"

"Some guy looking for his long-lost twin."

"Separated at birth?"

"Something like that. To be honest, it's hard to make out what the hell is going on. So far it's just a can of worms."

"Is that even worse than a kettle of fish?"

"Much worse. But I'll get it sorted."

The bartender planted two perfectly headed pints of Guinness behind Cora. She pulled a ball of money from her front pants pocket and teased a wrinkled ten out of it, passed it to the bartender, and turned back with the glasses in her hands.

McBride took his and said, "What about you?"

"What about me?"

"What brings you to town?"

"How do you know I'm not local?"

"I can tell."

"Looking for work."

"What kind of work?"

"Insurance. Life, home, and auto." She looked embarrassed. "I know, right? I *am* the world's dullest bitch. Somebody should arrest me. Sláinte!"

They saluted their pints and drank a long draught.

She wiped the foam from her upper lip with the back of her free hand. "You don't look like a private investigator."

He looked himself up and down and shrugged his shoulders. "I don't look like a cowboy either." Then looked her up and down and said, "You don't look like an insurance agent."

"Thanks," she said. "I try not to."

"There's more to it than that though, isn't there?"

"More to me, you mean?"

"Maybe the insurance gig pays the bills, but it's not your passion, is it?"

"For God's sake, insurance a passion?"

"Like that guy in Groundhog Day. What was his name?"

"Yeah. Ned something. I work for that guy."

"I thought you were job hunting?"

"If you worked for Ned Somebody wouldn't you be job hunting?"

"Point taken. So what is it then, your passion?"

She thought hard about it for a few seconds. "Crossword puzzles?"

He laughed — a little too hard. Something about the way she offered this hypothesis cracked him up.

"What's so funny about crossword puzzles?" she said in mock offense.

"Nothing. Just not what I was expecting. I thought maybe rodeo clown or tightrope walker or belly dancer."

"So something in the entertainment business. Pole dancer, you were hoping."

He laughed again and gulped another long draught to calm his nerves. "Seriously now. I'm interested."

"What about you? Your life is your job?"

"It is when I'm working."

"How often is that?"

"It varies. Could work twenty-four seven if I wanted to join an agency, but I like being my own boss."

"And I'm going to guess your hobby is painting. I bet your place is full of kitschy acrylics."

"You're close actually. It's scuba diving."

"No, really?"

"No. When I'm not working I like to drink. And read books. And play chess and one-seat sculling."

"In that order?"

"There's no set order. OK, that's me. You've danced around long enough. Let's hear it."

"Photography."

"What do you shoot?"

"You know, people always ask that, and I never used to know how to answer. Now I just say, whatever the hell I want."

"Good on ya!" He offered a toast. After a swallow he said, "Gotta website?" He took out his phone and she typed in the web address. He stood close to her so they could look at it together. He felt her breast against his arm.

Black-and-white nature photography. Mostly forests and canyons and similarly shadowy setups. Moody and mysterious, but not depressing. There was a whole series called "Forest After Fire" that was very black and beautiful.

"This is good stuff," he said, and meant it. "You have an eye."

"Thank you!" she said, close to his ear. "It gets me out of the house."

"Where was the forest fire?"

"Oh, somewhere out in the sticks. I was just out driving and came on it."

"When I get home, I'm going to order a print of my favorite."

"I'll drink to that!" They tossed off the last of their pints. She bumped him with her hip. "Your turn to buy, cowboy."

CHAPTER 19

APPROACH

Föhn returned for a second set and launched into it with a will.

McBride stepped close to be heard over the music. They leaned together over the bar and looked at her photos and drank.

They swore an oath to party till last call, but by the end of the second set they decided the oath was null and void on account of potential indecency and departed arm in arm before the encore.

McBride flagged for a taxi with a twenty while Cora, laughing, cocked her hips at the curb and stuck out a thumb. In thirty seconds they had a ride. They argued, getting in, which of them got the driver's attention.

McBride told the driver that was his last twenty and told him to find a bank machine before it was exhausted. The driver spotted an ATM sign within sixty seconds, which was about three times longer than it took Cora to lock herself onto McBride in the back seat.

They tumbled out together and drunkenly addressed the bank machine, Cora standing behind him with her hands in his front pockets while he tried to navigate the touch screens.

"Is that a bankroll in your pocket?" she cooed in his ear. "Or you just happy to see me?"

"No, I told you, I'm tapped! That's why we're at a bank machine, dummy."

"Hm, good. I was hoping it wasn't just money."

Back in the taxi, McBride handed $200 to the cabbie and told him to drive, he didn't care where, as long as when the money was up they were standing in front of the Essex.

"We just want to enjoy the night and probably neck like a couple of teenagers, OK with you?"

The cabbie gave him a hard look through the rearview mirror, but said, "Sure thing, mister."

"I don't think he likes you," Cora said.

"He likes my two-hundred dollars though." He grabbed her and tickled her ribs on both sides. She shouted a laugh and twisted and arched between his hands and he felt her whole body tense and strong. She knocked his arms away, and he could tell that she knew how to handle herself.

"Getting hot back here!" she gasped, and rolled down the window on her side. He grabbed her again, but didn't tickle her, and for the next hour the vagabond cab crisscrossed Manhattan while they kissed and fondled and laughed and sucked the cold spring air in like hot dogs jumping in a fresh creek.

It was past 3:00 before they leapt naked into McBride's kingsize bed on the 12th floor of the Essex, but well short of 4:00 before they passed out tangled together in the wet spot.

CHAPTER 20

CONTEMPLATION

McBride woke up late the next morning. Light was flooding the room painfully. Cora was standing at the windows naked. She heard him stir and turned around.

"Good morning, sunshine," she said.

Her breasts were smaller than he'd estimated before he saw them, fine and firm for a woman of forty. She was very fair and freckled, and the skin over her sternum and throat blushed red when she was excited. She was an energetic lover, even rough, but playful and comfortable.

The window light around her was blinding. "You're not one of those chirpy morning people, are you?" he said, shielding his eyes.

She had wound her fine blond hair on top of her head and it glowed and shifted in the light like yellow wheat.

"I'm never chirpy," she said. "Morning or night."

He rolled onto his side and propped his head on his hand. "You look good enough to eat."

She smiled, conscious of his admiration. "Want to see a trick?" she said.

"Sure."

There were three pink roses in a vase on the table by the window. She took one out and lay its long stem carefully across her hard nipples. She took her hands away and held them out to either side palms up.

"Look, ma, no hands!" she said.

"You're a nut!"

"What do I look like?"

"Like a suspension bridge?"

"Oh, you're funny."

"Actually, standing like that, you remind me of a Chinese opera singer. Only naked."

She bounced her heels off the floor, shaking the rose loose.

He gave her a clap. "What a performance!"

She took a bow and picked up the rose and said, "Check out time is noon, Mick. Let's roll." She'd taken to calling him "Mick" sometime last night.

They got in the shower together. She tried fooling around but he was too old and too hungover and too sleep-deprived to really get going again so soon. She just laughed playfully. That was the sexiest thing about her.

CHAPTER 21

BITING THROUGH

Over breakfast in the West Gate Tavern, Cora announced around a bite of cinnamon croissant that she'd had an idea: "Suppose I wen up a Bosson wih you?" She swallowed and explained: "I can look for work there as well as here."

McBride was a little stunned.

She saw it. "I know. Just a thought. But I was thinking of going back home anyway."

"Where's home?"

"Albany."

"I know Albany a little."

She shrugged. "It's as good a place as any to freeze your tits off." She looked down at her coffee — "Anyway forget I said it," — then up at him again.

Damn but she had pretty eyes. Not in the usual way — big, dark, and sultry. They were small, sky blue, bright, and hard.

"No, it's not that," he said, without knowing what *that* was exactly. "But are you sure?"

"Why do I have to be sure?"

That was a fine point.

"Did you drive down?" she said.

"Yeah. Do you have a car?"

"I can get it later." She answered quickly. She'd been thinking about it already.

McBride took a hit off his coffee and mulled her offer.

"Albany," he said. "Last time I was in Albany, must have been five years ago. I drove over with the DA to depose an informant at the Facility."

"Well you've seen the highlights then."

"Fraud case. You ever get involved in that kind of thing?"

"Fraud? No. I'm just a records analyst. — Anyway, listen, Mick, forget what I said about Boston. I just got excited. I do that."

He smiled at her. "No, I think it's a swell idea. You just surprised me."

"Seriously?"

"Well, not *seriously* seriously. But sure. Why not? Let's have some fun."

They made arrangements to meet again in a couple of hours. Cora said she needed to get her stuff from her girlfriend's where she was staying in Brooklyn. McBride needed to annoy a few more service staff with Gray's picture.

CHAPTER 22

GRACE

They met in the Essex lobby. McBride was sitting on a couch. He watched her cross the room to him. She walked like a woman who walked a lot in shoes that weren't heels on ground that wasn't paved. Long smooth swinging confident strides. Hips that made you feel a little weak in the chest. A lot of pretty women were just pretty. Cora had solid grace.

He stood and gave her a hug. "You changed your shirt."

"Yeah." Cora smiled her crooked smile. "It needed it." The fresh shirt was a fluffy loose-fitting white blouse that she wore unbuttoned down to her bra.

"This all you have?" he said.

She was pulling a clean red overnight bag behind her. "Yup. I'm set. For a couple of days anyway. Where's yours?"

"I'm wearing it. Have toothbrush," (he patted the left sleeve pocket of his fishing jacket with his right hand) "will travel."

He offered to pull the bag for her. It was light.

"Do you have a gun too?" she said as they headed outside.

"Why?"

"Just wondered."

"I mean why carry one?"

"I don't know. Habit?"

The doorman waved a taxi up and the driver tossed Cora's bag in the trunk.

McBride said, "Bronx station."

She snuggled up to him in the back seat, kissed him, then turned away and leaned against him, looking out the window.

"This is a wonderful town."

"Yup." He rested his chin on her silky hair.

She lifted one arm over her head and caught the back of his neck in the palm of her hand. "You need a shave."

He wrapped his arms around her, letting one hand come to rest on her breast. It was a nice fit.

The taxi crept along in sunny afternoon traffic. Manhattan always reminded him of China's peculiar granite-column mountains. Like rafting down a lazy river between cliffs of fire.

"This guy you're looking for," she said. "How did he come to lose his brother?"

"The story is they were separately adopted at birth."

She angled her face up. "You don't sound convinced. What do you think's the real story?"

"I don't know."

"Well, how do you find who you're looking for if you don't know the real story?"

"And that, darlin', is the fine art of detecting."

"Uh-huh. What do you know about him so far? Do you even know his name?"

"Nope."

"But you thought he might be in New York?"

"Not really. Mostly just checking out the back story."

"Did it check out?"

"Nope."

"Think you're being conned?"

"Not sure. Probably not."

"So what is it then?"

"Don't know yet. Have to finesse it."

"Crazy kind of a job."

"It's a living. The superior man is patient and perseveres. Eventually all the pretty pieces fall together."

CHAPTER 23

SPLITTING APART

Later, weaving up I-95, Cora asked him if had an office in Boston like a real detective.

"You're sitting in it."

"This?"

"This."

"No typewriter?"

"No but there's a bottle of scotch in the glove box."

She didn't check. "It's the best damn private detective's office I've ever seen."

"How many have you seen?"

"One. But I like it. Especially the empty Doritos bags in the back."

"It suits me."

"Yes it does. Can't picture you in anything else." She stroked the dashboard experimentally, leaving a smudge in the dust. "I guess you work alone then?"

"Mostly."

"Mostly?"

"I have a friend who helps me out with research and so on."

"What's her name?"

"I didn't say it was a she."

"No, but what's her name?"

"Sylvia. Why? Jealous?"

"Why would I be jealous? Is it strictly business?"

"Mostly. Not strictly."

Cora chewed on that for a minute, then said, "I never asked you if you were married."

"I never asked you either."

"What if we're cheating?"

"Would you like that?"

"No. Have you ever been cheated on?"

"Probably."

"So you were married?"

"Is there a stain?"

"Only a little one."

"What about you?"

"Nope. Not interested," she said. "So what happened? If you don't mind me asking."

"What happened? It wasn't that something particular happened. It just slowly sort of came apart. The little house of our happiness. We didn't even notice it happening really. And then one day the roof fell in. And that was that."

"But you think she was stepping out?"

"There were signs. When you do this kind of work, you — I guess I didn't really want to know. What difference would it make? We were over either way. Fuck it."

"Yeah," Cora said, "there's still a little stain."

CHAPTER 24

RETURN

McBride and Cora got back to his place in Peabody around dinnertime. McBride gave her the penny tour: the place was basically two rooms, a bath, and foyer: bedroom and bath upstairs, living/kitchen down, porch in the back, overlooking the lake. He took a flyer from under a magnet on the refrigerator and asked her to call for a pizza — or whatever she wanted.

"I need to get some exercise. I'm going for a quick row before it gets too dark." He called over his shoulder as he was ducking out the back, "There's beer in the fridge. Help yourself."

Upside down across two sawhorses off the porch there was a scratched-up black fiberglass single-seat sculling shell and two oars. He hoisted it overhead and trotted it down to the short dock.

It was already dusk. He jumped in and pulled away hard, angling across the lake. It was only a couple of hundred yards to the opposite shore where there was a little community pier. He drove his boat straight onto the bank next to the pier and hopped out.

Sylvia's place was set back a little through the trees of the narrow shoreline park. The lights were off. Usually he'd just go up to the back door, but tonight he was cautious. He circled around to the front and found her car in the drive, a powder blue Prius. He went up to the front door and gently tested the knob. Locked. He rang the doorbell and listened. Not a sound.

He took his phone out and tried to call her again.

Again she didn't answer.

He texted her: — *i'm at your place. where are you*

No response.

He jogged back through the trees and ran his shell back into the water. A hawk was turning loops above the water, dodging a pair of harassing grackles. The sun was setting but he needed to clear his head so he pulled a couple of laps around the lake before turning in to his place again.

He found Cora sitting in one of the Adirondack chairs on the porch, drinking a beer. She waved at him as he came from the dock with his shell overhead.

"Good row?" She lifted her beer. "I brought one for you too."

He laid the boat belly up across the sawhorses and came up the porch and sat down in the other chair where a bottle of Guinness was waiting.

"I ordered a meat-lover's pizza. OK?"

"Sure. Whatever."

She turned in her chair and leaned toward him. She'd taken her bra off under her shirt. "What shall we do tonight?"

"Well, I need to work later."

"On your case?"

"Yeah."

"Can I come?"

"No, sorry. It's confidential. Anyway, I'm not heading out till after midnight."

"Wow. What kind of private detecting do you do at that hour?"

"Nothing like that. Just have to meet with someone."

"Come on, Mick, give a girl some cloak-and-dagger."

"Really, it's nothing. Just need to go have a chat."

"About your New York trip?"

He changed the subject. "So what's your plan tomorrow?"

"For what? You mean for job hunting? Oh, I got some moves I can make, some angles I can work." She rocked her chin back and forth as she said it.

McBride laughed. "Aren't you the operator."

"I know some people who know some people in Boston. I'll start calling around."

"Are you going to need wheels?"

"Probably not tomorrow."

"See how it plays out then?"

"Right."

"So how'd you get into the insurance business?"

"It's not a business. It's a job. Actually I just answered an ad in the paper."

"What business would you rather be in?"

"I think I'd like to run my own crime family."

"I hear that's a tough line of work to break into."

"I don't know, I don't think about stuff like that."

"What stuff do you think about?"

"I don't know. I'm not a thinker. I'm a doer. I like to be busy. Don't you?"

The pizza arrived with a bang on the front door. McBride went through and brought it back with two more Guinness.

Twenty minutes later Cora had him upstairs in bed.

CHAPTER 25

INNOCENCE

She sat up between his knees without taking her hands from his dick, her breasts squeezed between her arms. "What the hell are you doing?"

He had his phone in his hands, aiming it at her. "Taking your picture, baby." He was also setting an alarm to wake himself up later.

She grinned and frowned at once. "Don't let that fall into the wrong hands."

"Same to you," he said, nodding at her squirming hands.

"I mean it, Mick." She yanked his dick hard enough to hurt.

"Ow!"

"I *mean* it."

"Don't worry," he said innocently. "I'm a good boy."

. . .

He needed the alarm. He woke up feeling clammy and limp, his phone clanging and buzzing on the bedside table. He and Cora were sprawled in a state of nature end to end on the bed. The ceiling fan hummed faintly in the darkness above the bed.

In the bathroom he messaged Sylvia again. Still no reply.

When he returned the lamp was on and Cora was sitting up on the side of the bed, wiping her face with her tough little hands. She had covered her shame in lace panties while he was out of the room. "What time is it?"

"One."

"Can I ride along?" She looked around the bed for her other clothes. "I can wait in the car. I don't mind."

"Not this time," he said, pulling his shirt on still-buttoned over his head. "Get some sleep."

"I feel funny staying here by myself." She had found her shirt between the bed and the table.

"I won't be long," McBride said. "An hour or so." He gave her a kiss on the forehead.

"Sure?"

"Sure."

She pulled his mouth down to hers and caught his balls in her hand. He pulled away before it was too late. She lay back on the bed and watched him finish dressing.

CHAPTER 26

THE TAMING POWER OF THE GREAT

McBride drove around to Sylvia's place first. No lights on and her car was still parked in the drive.

He headed down 93 to Boston, but not to the Taj. Instead he put the Office in the garage at South Station and flagged a taxi down with a hundred-dollar bill.

He read the driver's name off his hackney license on the dash. "Your name is Durante? Like Jimmy Durante?"

"That's me. Gene Durante. No relation."

"No, I didn't think you looked Italian."

Gene was black.

"Where you headed?"

McBride offered the bill over the seatback, saying, "Listen, Gene, I've got to pick somebody up at the Park Plaza and bring them back here. It might take a while. If you can hang out with me for a couple of hours, there's this one and another one in it for you. Deal?"

Durante snapped the bill away and smiled into the rearview mirror. "At a hundred an hour, I can hang out all night, mister."

"Outstanding. Fire this chariot up!" He was in a great mood. Things were finally happening.

.   .   .

As they approached the Plaza, McBride said, "What I need you to do, drop me off like normal in the front drive. Then head out. Drive around for a while. Go to an all-night Dunk's. Whatever. Come back and pick me up here at three-thirty. I'll probably be with a woman. Take us back to South Station." He flashed another bill in the mirror. "Here's the other hundred I'll hand you when you pick me up."

He walked straight through the lobby of the Plaza and down the hall and out the back entrance, then down the street and into the Four Seasons, through the foyer and lobby and out the front onto Boylston Street, then cut through the Garden and came out through the gate across from the Taj. *Sicut patribus, sit deus nobis.* God be with us as he was with our fathers. Bicycling and rollerblading prohibited.

At 02:00 sharp he knocked on Gray's door on the eighth floor.

Gray opened within three seconds, like he'd been watching for him. He was wearing a floor-length midnight-blue embroidered dressing-gown that reminded McBride of Gary Oldman's Dracula, and smiling like a horse. "The prodigal detective returneth! How was New York?"

"Lovely."

Sylvia was perched atop the round dining table, one bare foot propped on one of the sitting chairs, the other leg crossed over it. One arm rested over the knee, holding an empty martini glass limply. She was wearing shorts and a T-shirt, revealing her elegant tattoos above knees and elbows. Her eyelids hung like curtains. She was drunk.

Gray took her glass as he passed her on the way to the bar where he started mixing a new set of drinks.

"Hey, McBee. Gimme a ride home?" She smiled, perhaps self-consciously.

"Sure," McBride said.

"You missed your check-in last night, Mr. McBride," Gray said over his shoulder.

"I was working."

"At two in the morning?"

"I'm working now at two in the morning."

"Indeed."

McBride sat down in the chair Sylvia didn't have her feet on and waited for his martini.

"Have a good trip?" she said.

"Some good, some bad. I've been trying to reach you for two days."

"I know. I wasn't in the mood. You annoyed me."

"Sorry."

"I'm over it now."

"Glad to hear it."

Gray came from the bar bearing the round lacquer tray with three martinis on board.

"What shall we toast?" he said, as they took their glasses.

"Truth?" McBride said.

"An ominous word," Gray said, taking the last glass and tossing the tray across the room onto the sofa. "I think I smell a scolding in the air."

"Well, if anybody can dish out a scolding," Sylvia said, "it is our man McBride!"

Gray lifted his glass. "To our man McBride then."

"Cheers!"

"Sláinte."

"*Now*," Gray said, steeling himself, "I'll need a seat for this. Dear?"

Sylvia took her foot from the chair and let her legs dangle, still crossed. She glanced at McBride to see if he'd noticed the endearment.

He had.

She affected unconcern.

He caught that too.

"Nobody at the Essex ever heard of you, Morris. I interviewed the hotel manager, the desk clerks, the doormen, the maids, the bartenders, the neighborhood panhandlers, and the pigeons across the street in Central Park. No one betrayed the slightest recognition of your name or your face."

Gray frowned unhappily. "I told you there was no point in going. Now we've lost two days. Do you have anything else to report?"

McBride laughed unhappily. "That's your response?"

Sylvia giggled.

Gray shrugged and exhaled impatiently.

"I thought," McBride said, "you might want to try a different story. The wheels have come off this one."

"I don't understand why it matters to you who I am. The job is to find the person in that photo."

"It matters because the person you're hiding from is the person in the photo."

"But it's not."

"Then who are you hiding from?"

"I can't tell you that. You wouldn't believe it if I did tell you."

"We already don't believe you," Sylvia said.

"Why can't you tell me?" McBride said.

Gray darkened and opened his mouth to answer, then stopped and looked away.

McBride waited impatiently.

Gray took a sip of his martini, and, still looking away, said, barely audibly, "I can't. I can't tell you the truth. I—" His voice broke. He rose suddenly and walked to the window at the back of the room and stood looking out.

McBride and Sylvia exchanged a look. He wanted to know if she knew anything. She didn't.

"I have a family, you see," Gray said, his voice rough, bouncing off the glass back into the room. "I have a wife and a daughter."

McBride saw surprise in Sylvia's face. She believed it.

"They — their lives are —" Gray was crying now. "Their lives depend on what I do here."

"What you do where?" McBride said.

Gray turned round again and looked up at them through eyes ringed with pain. "I can't explain why. Don't ask me. You're a much better detective than I am a liar. And I'm so tired. So tired of lying and making up lies. I can't tell you what you want to know, what you have every right to know. I can only tell you that the photo is real, and that I am running out of time to find him. I can't tell you anything else that will help you find him because I don't know anything else."

The way he said "him" had changed. "He" was the enemy now.

"I honestly do not have anything else to go on except that photograph," he continued. "That fucking photograph destroyed my life. Because of that photograph, I'm going to die very soon. All I want to do is make sure no one else dies too." Gray had slowly crossed back to them as he spoke and now sat down again exhausted. "All I'm asking," he concluded, "is that you do your best for the next week. It doesn't matter the cost. After that it won't matter."

McBride sat watching him for a minute, trying to make it make any kind of sense, but he couldn't do it, and he couldn't convince himself either that Gray's anguish was just an act. He couldn't get an angle on it. Finally, having nothing else to offer, he just said, "All right, Morris," and stood to leave.

Gray did not get up. He looked done in. All his barbs were blunted.

Sylvia slid off the table and hugged Gray's head against her stomach, looked around for her shoes, found them and tossed them into a large shopping bag that appeared to contain more of her things, then gave Gray another hug, but not a kiss, and left with McBride.

CHAPTER 27

THE CORNERS OF THE MOUTH

Sylvia spoke first, going down in the elevator, leaning back against the dark paneled wall and looking at McBride with the corners of her mouth drooping: "Yes," she said, "I fucked him." She was slurring a little. "So do I get a spanking?"

"If you like," McBride said. "Or how about a little caffeinated nourishment? I need you sharp if you can manage it. Something's up."

Confused, she concentrated her face. "Whut?"

"I think I'm being tailed."

She tried to focus. A grin came and went. Maybe it was a joke. "What do you mean?"

"What I said. I think someone is keeping an eye on me."

The elevator opened and they went into the lobby. He led her to a padded leather bench. "You'll need your shoes," he said. "We have to walk a bit. I wanted to make sure I wasn't followed."

She sat down heavily and dug for her shoes in the shopping bag. He sat beside her. He was pretty beat too.

"So how was it?" he said.

"How was what?" she said without looking up. "Oh, that."

"Did you learn anything?"

She wagged a hand back and forth. "It was kind of sweet. Kind of sad. The earth did not move."

"Did you learn anything?"

"He's so lonely," she said, not listening. "He cried."

"But you didn't know about the wife and the daughter, did you?"

She gave him a fairly fierce look, but he couldn't tell whether it was for him or for Gray. "No."

She got her shoes on and he took her arm in one hand and her bag in the other and led her out to the street.

"Now, don't look around," he said. "I'll take care of that. You just hang on me and stagger along in blissful contentment."

It didn't take much acting. She was smashed and half asleep anyway. She leaned on him heavily, holding onto his arm with both hands.

She felt warm against him in the cool night air. Now and then he put his cheek against the top of her head. It gave him a chance to glance back. But he liked doing it too. Once when he did it she squeezed against him and turned her face up and looked at him, and he almost kissed her, and he thought she wanted him to, but he saw the drink in her sleepy eyes, and he felt queer about it, so he just bumped her forehead with his and whispered, "You OK?"

"Hmm," she mumbled drowsily. Then, with deliberation: "I'm fine."

"Good."

Softly: "See anything?"

"No."

"But you think there is someone?"

"Probably not right now."

"You have your gun." She felt it under his arm.

"Just in case."

He walked her around the corner of the Public Garden, along Boylston Street. The streets were so still. A fine layer of mist stretched out above the surface of the pond in the Garden. He was enjoying himself immensely. It was more than just the excitement of eluding a possible chase. He wished he could walk her around till dawn, hanging on his arm. He loved this city.

He walked her through the Four Seasons lobby and out the back, then around the corner to a 24-hour Dunkin' Donuts on Charles Street where he bought her an espresso. She slumped open-mouthed in her seat across from him and drank it between both hands.

"You're pathetic," he said.

"Fuck you, McBee."

"Fuck you back."

"Are we ever going home tonight?"

He checked the time on his phone. "Yeah. Drink that up and we'll go."

They staggered on up Charles a block or so then doubled back to the Plaza, as though they were too drunk to notice where they were. He saw no hint of pursuit.

Durante was already there, standing against his cab smoking a brown cigarette and telling jokes with a security guard. He made like he was happy to see them and opened the door for them. McBride stuck the hundred in his hand and told him to go the wrong way for a while and come back to South Station from across the river.

Durante jammed the bill into a front pocket and grinned and opened the door for them. "Whatever you say, mister."

CHAPTER 28

THE PREPONDERANCE
OF THE GREAT

McBride poured Sylvia into the back seat and climbed in after.

"Where's the Office?" she said.

"South Station."

"So who's following you?" she said.

"I don't know yet. That's what I need you for."

"Well, how — I mean, why — *when* — Fuck! I'm drunk as hell."

"Yes, you are."

Sylvia slid down in her seat and put her head back.

"Don't go to sleep now, pal. Tell me what happened while I was in New York."

"When did you leave?" she said to the roof. "Was it just yesterday?"

"Almost two days now."

"He came to my house in a limo."

"What time?"

"I don't know. What time did you call? It wasn't early, but I was still asleep anyway. These nights are killing me. You know I'm a morning person. I can't go on like this. I can't even keep track of the time lately."

"Did he call first?"

"If he did I didn't hear it, but I don't think he did. — He couldn't have. He doesn't have my number."

"But he has your address."

"Hey!" She lifted her head. "How did he — You must have told him."

"The hell I did."

She tossed her head sideways, frowning. "Why didn't I think about that before now?"

"Swept you off your feet." He'd never seen her this drunk before. "So then what?"

"We drove. He had a mini-bar in the car. He told the driver to wander up the coast. Seriously, it's stunning how much he drinks."

"Did you stop for lunch?"

"It's not the amount. It's the regularity. It's like every hour on the hour. For two days."

"Did you stop for lunch?"

"Though I guess that still adds up to quite a lot."

"Stay with me, Syl. Did you stop for lunch?"

She broke out laughing. "We did McDonald's drive-thru! In a stretch limo! He thought it was *fascinating*. He said it was very" (she fingered air quotes) "'twentieth century.'"

"What did you talk about?"

"Oh, I don't know."

"Did he talk about himself?"

She made an effort to remember, knitting her brow. "No. No. Nothing."

"Well?"

"We talked about me. He wanted to hear my life story."

"What an operator."

"No, McBee." Her tone was admonitory. "You don't get it. He's sincere. I mean, I know he's batshit. But he's honestly batshit."

"All right. He's sincere and he's honest and he's crazy. What else? You drove up the coast a while, and then?"

"We headed back to the city after a while. I had to ask to stop to pee. He told the driver to locate the finest restroom in Maine. Like this is something a driver could know."

"Maine!"

"Yes. I couldn't tell if he was kidding or clueless. We turned around after that."

"So where was the best shitter in Maine?"

"A truck stop, of course. Jason said we needed gas anyway. But Morris made him drive through three different places before he found one he thought was good enough for me. I thought I was going to piss myself."

"I meant what city."

"Somewhere near Portland. We drove along the coast mostly."

"You said that. What time was that?"

"Three-ish. Four-ish." She was still slurring a little. It sounded like "Threesh, forsh."

"Jason was your driver's name?"

"Yeah."

"Did you get the last name?"

"No. I really wasn't thinking about being on the job. I was enjoying myself."

"Did you get the feeling Morris had hired him before?"

"I don't know. Sorry."

"Did Morris hit the head too?"

"No. He never got out of the car from the time we left my place till we got back to the Taj. He had to go though. He went straight to the toilet when we got to the room."

"Is he afraid of public restrooms?"

"Aren't you?"

"How long were you out of the car?"

"In the restroom? I don't know. As long as it takes to use the toilet in a truck stop."

"Well, was it a number one or a number two?"

She rolled her head toward him without lifting it. "Five or six minutes. Weirdo."

"Did you do any shopping?"

"Shopping?"

"Beef jerky. Refrigerator magnets. Condoms."

"No…" She drawled it out in warning.

"What time did you start making out?"

"Fuck you."

"Come on, Syl. I need to know."

"Fuck you need to know."

"Look, I'm trying to put the timeline together, what was going on here and what was going on in New York." This was partly true. Also, he just wanted to know.

"*Nineteen-thirty hours,* captain." She tried to bite it out, but she was a little too slack-jawed to make it sting.

"OK, but seriously, is that anywhere close to being right?"

"We got back around six or seven. He hit the head and then he called down and told the concierge to find us an excellent meal and have it sent up."

"Did you go out again?"

"No. Not till breakfast." Her mouth twisted a little around that, betraying her determination to sound indifferent. She frowned.

"Were you together the whole time yesterday? Could he have made any other calls?"

"I don't know."

"Think, Syl. He called me on your phone yesterday noon. He called the concierge from the room phone around dinnertime. Did he use your phone again?"

"No."

"Did he use the room phone again?"

"Not that I remember. I don't think so."

"Maybe he called down for ice? A midnight snack?"

"No."

"Did you run out of ice?"

"No."

"Did he use any of his burners?"

"No."

"Maybe while you were in the bathroom?"

"How would I know? If he wanted to make a call without me knowing about it I suppose he could have done it."

"Were there any visitors?"

"No."

"What about the person who brought dinner up?"

"Well, all right, there was one visitor. Enough interrogation. Tell me what you're driving at."

"Did you tell him I was in New York?"

"Yes."

"When he showed up at your place?"

"Yes."

"What was his reaction?"

"Pissed off."

"What was the discussion? Walk me through it."

"I was still in bed. I heard the doorbell and looked out the window next to the bed and saw the limo out front."

"OK, so you come to the door in your panties, and…?"

"So I put a shirt on and went down. I wasn't wearing panties if you want to know. But it's a long shirt. It's blue. There's a puppy on the front."

"Really?"

"No."

"Was Morris at the door himself, or was it the driver?"

"Morris. Driver stayed in car."

"Weren't you surprised to see who it was?"

"I figured he was looking for you. I was sleepy. The first thing I said when I opened the door was, 'McBee is in New York.' It knocked the smile right off his face."

"I bet it did. What did he say?"

"He wanted to know why we didn't show at two. I said, Ask McBride."

"How did he wind up calling me on your phone?"

"I let him in and he said he wanted to take me to lunch and asked if he could use my phone to call you. I gave—"

"Why didn't he use his own phone?"

"I didn't ask."

"Did he have one? Did you see one on him or in the car?"

"I didn't."

"So you gave him your phone."

"Yes, and went to the bathroom. When I came out he was standing in the middle of the living room talking to you."

"Funny, I figured he was lying about you being in the head."

"He's not a bad person, McBee. If you'd come down off your — Never mind. So what happened in New York?"

"Well, I got laid."

Sylvia affected a shattering double-take. "Wow. Have you sold the movie rights yet?"

"I've had some feelers."

"So who was the lucky girl? — Girl, right?"

"Woman."

"Whatever."

"She's the tail."

"You got a piece of — Oh." It took a couple of seconds for her to work it out. "Wait. You didn't get laid, you got played? McBee, you're losing your touch."

"Yeah well, I figured it out eventually."

.   .   .

At South Station they walked through from Atlantic Avenue up to the parking building and recovered the Office. McBride made Sylvia walk up the stairs to wake her up.

Back in the Office, she said, "OK, so what's the plan?"

"You're going to follow her follow me."

"How's that work?"

"When I dump her, she'll go to see her employer. You'll tag along."

"She's here?"

"She came back with me. She's job hunting."

"No shit? Where is she now?"

"I left her at my place."

"You dog."

"I know."

"So what do you think it's about?"

"That's why I was grilling you about your day with Morris. I thought it was possible he hired a second private eye to keep an eye on the first private eye. But the timeline doesn't work. Morris didn't know I was in New York until you told him around noon yesterday. I spotted Cora in the bar around ten that night. It sounds like Morris never had a chance to call anyone. Even if he already had someone on the hook for the job, they wouldn't be in New York, and it's not likely they could get there, find me, and follow me to the bar in that time."

"It's maybe doable. *If* he called someone right away."

"Maybe. Are you sure he didn't use your phone again? Maybe he made another call while you were in the bathroom?"

"He was talking to you when I came out. Remember, he put me on with you? And he didn't know exactly where you were in New York unless you told him, because I didn't."

"No, but the Essex would be the obvious place. Anyway, even if he could have gotten someone onto me that fast, why would he?"

"Because he's paranoid."

"And even then, why would the tail pick me up in a bar? The whole idea is *not* to get made."

"OK, so how do you know it wasn't a legit seduction? You're not that ugly."

"I didn't know it at the time. I worked it out later. For example, she asked me when we met what brought me to town. How did she know I was from out of town? Then yesterday morning out of the blue she invited herself back to Boston with me. "

"Wow, you *did* get laid!"

"Yeah, but she has a car in New York. She says she can go back for it. But seriously? Who would do that? So we arranged to meet up in a couple of hours so she could collect her things or whatever. She told me she'd been staying with a friend for a couple of months. When she came back to the hotel she was pulling a little red carry-on bag. I picked it up, it was practically empty, and it looked brand new. And she had on a new shirt. It was still wrinkled in the shoulders. It was too big for her and it didn't go with her style. She was wearing a worn denim shirt when I met her, the new shirt was a blousy white silky thing. I think somebody bought it for her. I think she followed me to New York. I'm guessing she doesn't have a car there at all. She rode down with whoever bought that shirt and suitcase. And she's been real interested in hearing about my case. I told her when we met that I was a detective."

"Anybody would want to know about that though."

"Anybody would and they'd just ask me straight out. She's interested but indirect, like she doesn't want to make me suspicious. And she keeps coming back to it. Another thing is she talks like someone who's used to being lied to. She catches little things and follows up on them. Like she knows how to interrogate people who are hiding something."

"You left her at your place. But you still think we're being followed?"

"Probably not. Just being safe. But I figure the car is bugged."

"You're serious."

"I can't figure how else they stayed with me all the way to New York without getting burned."

"Did you check?"

"No. I wouldn't do anything about it anyway."

"So they don't know you're onto them."

"Exactly."

"OK, so what's it all about? If it isn't Morris keeping tabs on you, then…?"

"Then who else would want to know what I was up to? If it isn't the guy who hired me to find a guy, it must be the guy he hired me to find."

"Or it's just a coincidence."

"This is my only case. If it's not about a case, why would anyone be following me? That costs real money."

"But that means the brother is real."

"I know it seems incredible."

"Why didn't you tell Gray about this?"

"Do you believe Gray's latest story?"

"About him having a family and their lives hanging on whether you find the prodigal brother? Sounds like something out of a gangster flick."

McBride nodded. "But he did seem genuinely in distress."

"So like the bad guys are holding his wife and kids hostage in a basement somewhere in Southie and they're gonna whack 'em unless he gives up his brother? You're the cop. Do you believe it?"

"*Was* the cop. I believe he believes it, or something as bad."

"But you don't, or you would have told him about your new girlfriend. What's her name?"

"The name she gave me is Cora Lobb. And it's probably legit since it was also the name on the website she showed me."

"Website?"

"Photography. Reminds me, I've got a picture of her on my phone. I'll send it to you. I was hoping you could do some digging online tonight."

Sylvia moaned heavily. "*Hell* no. I'm absolutely shitfaced and fagged out and it's half past fuck in the morning."

CHAPTER 29

THE ABYSMAL WATER

Cora woke McBride with a kiss at 10:00 o'clock. "I made you breakfast."

It took him a few minutes to get his body above his feet. She left him to struggle with the challenge alone. He found her on the porch, where she'd set out coffee and toasted bagels and lox and cream cheese and cantaloupe slices.

"Will you marry me?"

"Sure," she said. "I didn't have anything scheduled today."

Then he thought better of it. "It was a rhetorical question," he said sourly. "What about the job hunt?"

Cora mocked him with a frown. "Oh, I've been making some calls this morning. While you were sleeping. How did your meeting go last night?"

"Fine." He kept his tone curt. "What did you do while I was out?"

"I slept, of course."

He seized a bagel and assaulted it with a dollop of cream cheese.

The morning was dark and overcast. The lake lay murky and still below the yard. Abyssals of grey above and below.

"So what's your plan today?" she said.

He looked at the time on his phone. "Got some research to do. Then we'll see."

"Can I help?"

"First thing though is to wake up and get some exercise."

"Rowing?"

"Sculling," he grumbled.

She stopped talking and studied him eating.

He gulped his coffee aggressively and bit off hunks of bagel.

"Did I say something?" she said.

He answered without looking at her. "No."

She let it go, stood, and leaned out over the rail. "Dreary day for boating."

.   .   .

He laid the shell on the back of the water next to his dock and gated the oars into their locks and stepped in and pushed off gently. He crouched forward and caught the water in his blades and pulled away strong and smooth, feeling the warm energy flow through his thighs and arms and back. The water shot below him at first. Then smoothed away. Slowed. Stopped. Dissolved into vacuum. Above and below, both lake and sky spread out flat, featureless, and opaque. The spectral air between them felt empty, silent, and cold. The lake seemed to swallow every sound — the swish of his paddles, the slide of his seat, the drag of his breath. The treebound hilly shores moved, not him. He saw them passing, but felt no propulsion. He loved the release of this slick silence. The simple machinery of the boat carried him onward unchanged and unseen through time. The world glided around him. The wake of his passing expanded behind him in a supple V. Back to front he slipped into a trackless future, visible only going away, never coming on. Feeling forward, knowing backward. Afterthoughts. Afterimages. Aftertastes. Causes never noticed till after their effects. Pieced together in the sequel. Rhythming through. Stroke on stroke. Drive and recovery and drive again. Breath and breath. Reaching forward, leaning back. Surging and resurging. Knifing through on stiffened wings across a boundless silent pool. We only know the wake of action, never the now of it. We infer, from what recedes, our selves — never catching what we are, but only what we must have been to leave so long and wide a waving. Plotinus. We dream we are the vertex where the wake arises, not the point to which it aims. Falling backwards into history. Ahead of momentum, in back of awareness. Above and below, the luminous two-faced waters re-echoing each other.

▪ ▪ ▪

He pulled a few laps of the lake then angled in to Sylvia's dock. He knew she wouldn't be awake. He let himself in and yelled down the hall.

"Rise and shine, Syl!"

There was no response.

He put her coffeepot to work, banging around extra loudly in the kitchen, then yelled again.

A few minutes later, roused by the coffee, she shambled forth in bare feet and a long T-shirt. No puppy. She didn't look at him. "Fuck, McBee."

"Yeah. Coffee." He shoved a cup of black across the counter to her.

She picked it up as she passed by into the living room where she folded herself into the bowl of a massively ugly leather chair. It had been her father's chair, left to her when he went to Rome: high clover-shaped back, low seat, gold buttons, tufts about a yard deep, long feet like the rails of a time machine. She curled her legs up and held the hot coffee between her cold hands.

McBride came from the kitchen and sat on the arm of the sofa close to her.

"I e-mailed that picture to you."

"What picture?" Her voice was pretty rough.

"My new girlfriend. Remember?"

She nodded vaguely.

"I took a picture of her yesterday while — yesterday." He had cropped out everything below the shoulders before sending it. "So you'll know what she looks like. Long wavy blond hair, five-five, hundred-thirty-five pounds, forty years old. She's wearing blue jeans and that same white blouse. I put everything I think I know about her in the e-mail. Also a pic of her driver's license. Massachusetts, not New York. Address in Winchester."

Sylvia mumbled something unparsable.

"Do your tai chi," he said, "and get your blood circulating, you'll feel better."

She took a hot gulp of the coffee and leaned her head back, stretching her long neck back. "How are we going to work this today?"

"Well, I've already started having a shitty day, even though she made me breakfast. I'll make sure it gets worse, and later I'll tell her she'd better head on back to New York. I'll drive her to South Station or call her a cab. Either way, you follow her. I'll message you when. You remember how to tail somebody?"

"Don't follow too close." She took another gulp.

"I better get back."

She opened her eyes without lifting her head and looked across at him. "Do you think this thing is going to get dangerous?"

"No, not if we behave correctly."

"Well, shit." She closed her eyes again.

CHAPTER 30

THE CLINGING FIRE

Having a lousy day was easy. McBride wanted to spend the day checking out Cora's cover, but he couldn't risk talking on the phone, and using the computer was dicey because she kept wandering around. He shielded his computer screen with irritable sighs and gestures, and let it escalate from there.

"Why are you so restless?" he said. "Sit down and read a book. There's a wall full of them." He waved dismissively at the floor-to-ceiling bookcases that surrounded the unlit fireplace.

Cora was washing the dishes. She stopped and stared at him.

He made a point of ignoring her.

She threw the sponge down on the sink without finishing the job, took a towel and, drying her hands, crossed through to the fireplace. "I could start a fire."

"No."

"Lots of tinder here," she gibed. It was all nonfiction: history, language, criminal and constitutional law, true crime and case histories, and several shelves devoted to philosophy, religion, mythology, and historical Christianity.

"No detective novels," she said.

He didn't answer.

She took down a translation of the New Testament. In the beginning was the Tao, and the Tao was with God, and the Tao was God. "You read Chinese?" she said.

"Yes."

"Where'd you learn that?"

"China."

"No kidding. When were you there?"

"I need to work."

"OK!"

. . .

An hour later he offered to take her to the train station.

"Fine," she said, "I'll get my shit together," and stomped up the stairs.

He went out on the porch and called Sylvia.

"It's on. I'm taking her to South Station."

"Do we have to do this? I feel like hell."

"Yes. You go on ahead and hang out near the Fitzgerald Street entrance. I'll stick nearby after I drop her. Probably head to a pub."

"Fine."

"Find anything out today?"

"Not a lot. The *Girl from Albany* isn't. Pennsylvania. Parents still live there. They raise dairy cattle."

"That's why she walks like a farmer."

"Probably has strong hands too."

"Now, now—"

"One sister, Tampa. No police record. Never married. No property. Good credit rating. I couldn't find any employment. Nothing to connect her to Morris."

"Good work, Syl."

"Not bad considering I've got the mother of all alcohol headaches."

"I'll make it up to you."

"I'm doing it for Morris."

"You really like him?"

"I think he—"

"Gotta run." Cora was coming back down the stairs.

CHAPTER 31

INFLUENCE

McBride made a left out of the tunnel and stopped in the pullout in front of the station. They had not spoken on the drive. He affected sullenness.

Now Cora turned to him. "Look, I don't know what I did, but I want you to know something." She paused for a response, but he offered none. "I really liked you."

Liked. Past tense. Disguised apology. "Thanks," he said flatly.

Her eyes glistened. "Could I—do you think I could have one more kiss?"

Without answering he leaned toward her, keeping his face stiff.

She cupped his cheeks between her hands and looked carefully into his eyes and kissed him softly.

It was too tender to be a lie. Data point.

She got out and opened the back door and took her bag from the back seat.

The car behind them honked.

McBride glanced back in the mirror.

Cora turned her head toward it, frowned, and flipped it off, then slammed both passenger side doors and turned away. She caught her toe on something and stumbled, a parting indignity.

McBride stayed at the curb just long enough to verify that she went inside the station. God, she had a helluva walk. She went in and he voice-dialed Sylvia: "She's coming in—"

"I see her."

"She might know what you look like, so—"

"Hang back. I know."

"Is she calling anyone yet?"

"I think she's crying."

It took him a few seconds before he was calm enough to respond. "OK, I'm heading for the pub. Keep me on speaker. I'm going over to South Boston."

He needed a place where he could hang out and monitor the chase, that wasn't too far away, with surface parking, and that wouldn't look to anyone who might be following him like he was doing anything but getting a drink and some lunch.

"She's coming out of the station," Sylvia reported, on speaker. "I didn't see her make a call, but she must have 'cause she looks like she's waiting for someone. She's not flagging a taxi."

McBride headed across Summer Street bridge into Seaport where there were several bars with nearby street parking.

"She's standing on the corner, watching the traffic," Sylvia said. "Yep, here's her ride, coming around the corner off Atlantic. White pickup. Ford. She's getting in. Driver is male. Bald."

"Make the plates."

"Can't see."

"Two-door?"

"Yes."

"Open bed?"

"Yes. — They're heading out, on Summer, your direction."

"Well, that settles that question."

"I'm following."

"Not too close."

McBride found an open parking spot and tucked the Office into it, then got out and slipped into a corner doorway at the end of the A Street overpass. He waited there, listening to Sylvia, till he saw the pickup drive by.

"Can you stay on them?" he said. "They'll probably just park and wait for me to move on. Sorry I can't ask you to join me. I'll try to be quick."

"No problem. I'm almost having fun. All this excitement is getting some of the sick out of my head."

He took the stairs down to A Street and walked half a block up to the Blue Light. Granite bar, steel stools, good shellfish. The place was moderately busy with the lunchtime business-casual crowd. He sat at the bar and ordered a tuna burger and a Guinness.

Sylvia texted him with the plate number.

—*you rock syl*

— *they parked a block down. Waiting*

—*k*

He called one of his friends in the DA's office to ask them to run the plate number. Friend called back a few minutes later with the particulars: 2010 Ford F-150, registered to Michael Joyce, address in Revere. He took it all down in his Moleskine.

CHAPTER 32

DURATION

Sylvia texted him every three minutes: — *still waiting.*

Then after about twenty minutes she called him.

"Are they moving?" McBride said. "I'm almost done."

"No, they got out. Somebody in a limo just stopped beside them. They're talking to him through the window."

"A limo?"

"I guess so. A black SUV, like a Suburban or something. Tinted windows."

"Why do you say it's a limo?"

"Because they're talking to the guy in the back seat. And it's definitely not a taxi."

"Get the plates?"

"I'll try."

"I'm getting a call. I'll call you back." He switched to the incoming call. Boston number, no other ID. "McBride."

"My name is Mike Joyce. I'm the one who's been following you." He had a calm firm no-nonsense kind of voice.

"Speak of the devil. I was just looking up your address, Mike. In Revere."

"My boss would like to introduce himself."

"I'm fine, thanks. Yourself?"

But Joyce wasn't that easy to rattle. "Would it be convenient to meet right now?" A pro.

"Sure. I'm at the Blue Light."

"How about some place more private?"

Bullshit. "How about I get a table. Should I go ahead and order a round of drinks? What's your drink? You sound like a whiskey man to me."

Pause while Joyce conferred with the boss.

McBride clicked off without waiting for an answer and called Sylvia back. "They're on their way here. I'm outnumbered. Get here as quick as you can."

"On my way."

"Don't wait to park legally."

There were no free tables. Two suits were yukking it up at a corner booth in the back. McBride carried his beer over, handed them each a friendly $100 bill to vacate, sat down, and waved at the waitress to come reset.

She didn't like it. "How many in your party?" she said, annoyed.

He handed her a bill too. "Not sure. Four, probably."

A minute later Sylvia bounced through the front door and walked quickly down the length of the place. "I'm blocking a drive," she said, sliding into the booth. "But looks like I beat the limo."

"Not by much." McBride nodded toward the front. A stocky sixtyish bald man came in and made straight for them.

"That's your tail," Sylvia said.

He was dressed in relentlessly unremarkable sweater and slacks.

"Mike Joyce," he said when he reached the table. He didn't move to sit down or shake hands or attempt to smile. "This is not a very convenient place to talk. Suppose we meet—"

"It's convenient for me. If your man wants to talk, here I am."

Joyce frowned. "Is it just the two of you?"

"Yes."

He took an accusing look around, then turned without speaking and headed back toward the door. Despite his costume the wait staff noticed him. They watched him cautiously, coming and going again.

"He doesn't like the setup," Sylvia said.

"Nope. And whoever he's looking out for, Gray is scared shitless of him, so fuck me if I let him choose the place he shakes my hand the first time."

"Have you called Gray yet?"

"No. I want to take some measurements first."

. . . .

A couple of minutes crept by.

Joyce came back in, took another hard look around.

The bartender said, "Can I help you?"

Joyce ignored him. A beefy crop-haired athletic type came in after him and took up a position by the door. He was followed through the door by Morris Gray's identical twin. Last but not least: Cora Lobb. Beefsteak remained by the door; Joyce led the rest of the party down the room toward McBride and Sylvia.

Joyce made the introductions. "This is Mr. John Brown. You know Cora."

"John Brown?" McBride said. "Seriously?"

"Yes," Brown said. "I don't know about *seriously*."

"Well, you might as well sit down anyway."

Brown looked radiant in an immaculate navy blue suit and black crewneck shirt, stylishly un-combed hair, and sporting a freshly un-groomed chin brush. He had a confident stride and an alert, even vigilant, demeanor. McBride cataloged him as an Ivy League mafia don.

"This is my friend Sylvia Conti," McBride continued. "But you already know that, of course."

Sylvia kept her expression noncommittal, but her magnificent eyes caught the light as she considered Brown.

"Nice to see you again, Cora," McBride said. "Been a while. Thirty-five, maybe forty minutes?"

Cora frowned a smile and avoided eye contact.

The Brown party slid in around the crescent booth bench: Sylvia and Cora were on the outside ends, McBride next to Sylvia, Joyce next to Cora, Brown in the middle. It was cozy. Brown was the mirror image of Gray, but better groomed and costumed — less style and more taste, less out of place — a little thinner and fitter, and, somehow, older. Mike Joyce looked vaguely familiar, but McBride couldn't place him. Most likely, as another private dick, he'd seen him around the trial courts or the dive bars.

Beside him now, Brown gave McBride a warm smile and took his hand. "It's a pleasure to meet you, Mr. McBride," he said. Even their voices rhymed — Brown's and Gray's — though their accents were out of sync. "And you as well, Miss Conti." He reached across McBride to take Sylvia's hand in both of his own. It was *very* cozy.

The waitress came and offered them drinks.

"Do you have champagne?" Brown said expansively. "Bring us two bottles of your best." Then to McBride and Sylvia: "Have you eaten yet? Let's eat, shall we? Everything's on me. Let's be friendly."

"I already had a sandwich," McBride said. "You all go ahead."

The waitress dealt a round of menus and took their orders.

When she'd gone, Brown said, "Now then, Mr. McBride. I gather you've been trying to find me."

"Oh?" McBride said. "I think you've gathered the wrong end of the nosegay there, chief. You've had your man here and your bitch six feet up my business several days running." He was pleased to see they didn't like his tone. The key thing now was to control the ball.

Brown relaxed back in his seat deliberately. He would not be drawn. "I understand you, Mr. McBride. — May I call you Christian?"

"Nobody calls me that. But you can drop the mister."

"Good. McBride. I had you followed because I needed to know who was looking for me."

"We have these things now called telephones, John. Maybe one of your people could show you how to use it."

"Maybe you could mind your manners," Joyce said, cool and quiet.

"Maybe you could mind your place."

Joyce started to square up, as much as a man can square up sitting in a crowded booth, but Brown, in a gesture of beneficence, lifted the first two fingers of his left hand, and Joyce settled right down again.

"All right," Brown said with a nod. "You like the direct approach. I respect that. I'll be direct. Who are you working for?"

"None of your damn business."

Joyce looked up again hard, and Brown again, with the slightest side-glance, calmed him right back. Meanwhile Cora like a clam was quietly folding herself away. Sylvia seemed poised — either to deliver a belly laugh or a throat punch. From his post by the door at the far end of the bar, Angus the Killer Cow glared at everything.

McBride wasn't sure how much of his own attitude was an act.

"I think it is my damn business," Brown said, "when a private detective is showing a photo of me around town. Now that seems reasonable enough, doesn't it?"

"I remember one time I wanted to know what my daddy had gotten me for Christmas. So I hired a whore to seduce him and a dick to follow him around town in a white Ford F-150, plate number—"

Joyce bridled again. "Now look, brother,—" But Brown silenced him with those two beneficent fingers.

Cora flushed.

Eagle-eyed Angus had spotted the tension and readied himself to take a run at them.

Brown smiled placidly and took a sip of his water, then looked at McBride curiously and said, "This prostitute that you hired to seduce your father, was that at the Christian mission in Xinjiang province?"

McBride's startle reflex betrayed him.

It got Sylvia's attention too.

"Did I pronounce it reasonably correct? Xinjiang." His run at Mandarin sounded something like "King Kong."

McBride inserted a twinkle in his eye and looked over at Joyce. "Have you been showing my picture around China, you dog?"

"Welcome to the show, *punk.*" There was no twinkle. Joyce had almost had enough. Another tweak or maybe two and he'd fall right off his professional discretion.

The waitress returned with two bottles of bubbly in two buckets of ice. McBride was surprised they even had wine pails in a lunch bar like this. She left the bottles and returned again with five champagne flutes. Brown let the conversation cool while he eyed and sniffed and gently tasted the wine, approved it with a wink, and watched while the waitress poured their glasses.

"Your food will be out shortly," she said.

"Thanks, darling," Brown said as she left. He resumed with McBride, "We've gotten off on the wrong foot. May I suggest a toast to a fresh start?" He put his glass forth like an offering — would anyone touch it?

Joyce reacted at once, of course. Heel, dog. Sylvia waited for McBride, then joined the toast with him. Cora's reticent glass barely lost contact with the tablecloth.

Brown turned to Joyce. "Mike, I want to have a private word with Mr. McBride now. Why don't the two of you wait for me at the bar. Take the second bottle with you."

Joyce and Cora slid away and perched themselves midway down the long bar. Brown, McBride, and Sylvia reapportioned the bench space amongst themselves. Joyce monitored them in the bar mirror.

The waitress spotted the change and came over to rearrange the place settings again. They were making her nervous. The bartender was keeping a wary eye on the proceedings too.

Brown apologized for the trouble they were causing.

"Are you somebody?" she said.

"Not at all. Just a businessman. But I have to go around with an entourage like this. What can you do? Everything has to be such a production and bother." He didn't look the least bit embarrassed. He waited until she'd finished and gone, and turned once again to McBride. "All right. Now how shall we proceed?"

McBride put his glass down but kept his hand on it. "How about we play a game of question-poker? You answer one, I answer one."

Brown smiled. "All right then. Deal. Or should I say, ante up."

"What's your home address?"

Brown gave him a street number in Weston — the wealthiest town in Massachusetts, just west of Boston along Mass Pike. McBride took out his notebook and wrote it down, but Sylvia was already looking up the property listing on her phone. She showed it to him. $8 million house in a $4 million neighborhood. Eight beds, eight baths, eight acres, eight-thousand square feet.

"The owner's name is Murray Alper," McBride said.

"It's listed in my attorney's name for tax reasons."

Sylvia started looking up Alper.

"My turn," Brown said. "Who are you working for?"

"Your brother."

Brown nodded and frowned. "As I suspected."

"My turn. When's the last time you saw him?"

Brown consulted a calendar on the ceiling of the pub. McBride recalled Gray affecting a similar gesture at breakfast ten years ago.

"1982. I was a sophomore in college. What name is he using now?"

"Pass. Ask another."

"You're not allowed to pass."

"You are if you're wearing plaid underwear. Ask another."

Sylvia groaned.

"What story did he give you?" Brown said. "About why he was trying to find me?"

"He said someone sent him a photo of you claiming it was the twin he never knew he had. He hired me to track it down." Since all of Gray's stories were bullshit, it hardly mattered which one he reproduced. "What's your real name?"

"John Brown. I think I'm winning this game."

"If you were using your real name, your brother wouldn't need me to find you."

Brown considered for a moment, tapped the stem of his glass with his fingernail. "Listen, McBride, I just want to get in touch with him again. Will you help me arrange a meeting?"

"Why should I?"

"I haven't seen him in thirty years. If you tell him we met, he'll probably just disappear again."

"What makes you think so?"

"You say he's afraid of me. He knows my name. He could have looked me up any time. Hiring a detective is crazy. He's paranoid and delusional."

"What's his real name?"

"It's my turn, isn't it? Will you help me?"

"Is that your question?"

"Have you told him yet that you've identified me?"

"I thought you said he already knows who you are?"

"He doesn't know that *you* know that. And maybe he's become so disordered that he doesn't even know it himself anymore. In any case, *have* you told him?"

"No."

"Then will you help me?"

"Now it's my turn. What's his real name?"

"Sam. Short for Salmon. When we were children I called him Sammy."

"What did he call you?"

"Johnny."

"Where did you live?"

"My turn. When did he first contact you?"

"Three weeks ago. Where did you grow up?"

Brown put up a traffic-stopping palm. "OK, I think I've told you enough, McBride. If you're not willing to help me, there's no reason to continue."

"I'm thinking about it. What if I say no?"

"Then we go our separate ways."

"That's it?"

"That's it."

The waitress returned with their meals. At the bar Joyce and Cora were just getting their plates too. Brown poured another round of drinks and asked the waitress to bring a third bottle.

"Convince me," McBride said when she'd gone.

"How?"

"Tell me a story I can believe."

"What don't you believe?"

"What can I believe? You gave me an address that belongs to somebody else. You gave me a John Doe name. I don't believe anybody calls one twin Plain John Brown and the other one Fancy Sammy Says."

"I was named after my paternal grandfather. He was named after our maternal grandfather."

Quick. And plausible.

The interrogation continued around mouthfuls of lunch:

"Parents' names?"

"Marshal and Jean."

"Maiden name?"

"Udko."

"Spelling?"

Brown spelled it. McBride scribbled in his notebook.

"What kind of name is that?"

"Polish."

"Where did you grow up?"

"Europe."

"Europe where?"

"Everywhere. We traveled constantly. My father was a gem and jewelry buyer. Amsterdam. Rome. London. Berlin. Zurich. Istanbul. Paris."

"Who did he work for?"

"He was an independent contractor."

"Were you adopted?"

"Did he tell you that?"

"Are you?"

"Of course not."

"How do you know for sure?"

"How do you?"

"Where did you go to college?"

"The International University in Geneva."

"When did you graduate?"

"1984."

"What did you study?"

"Business Administration."

"What do you do now?"

"Live and let live."

"Let me see your ID."

"I don't carry ID."

"Why not?"

"I don't need to."

"Where do you keep your money?"

"I have various accounts in Switzerland and Dubai and elsewhere."

"In your name?"

"More or less."

"What the hell does that mean?"

"It means my finances are very well managed."

"By who?"

"Is that enough? Will you help me?"

McBride took the hockey photo from his notebook and showed it to Brown. "When was this taken?"

"I have no idea."

"But it's you."

"Apparently."

"At a Bruins game against the Flyers."

"Apparently."

"And you were there?"

"I have been to many hockey games, yes. I have season tickets. Perhaps you'd like to go sometime?" He waited for an RSVP like he actually meant it.

"Maybe," McBride said.

"But I've never seen that photo."

"Who are the women with you?"

"Let's leave them out of it."

"Who are they?"

"Friends."

"Old pals from college in Zurich?"

"You mean Geneva, don't you?" Brown let McBride see he knew he'd been trying to trip him up.

"All right, how do you see this meet up working?"

Brown beckoned for Joyce to return to the table. He came back, drink in hand. Cora stayed at the bar, looking away. McBride caught the bartender exchange a look with the waitress. She shook her head slightly. Would the musical chairs game never end?

McBride dictated most of the rules of engagement: no prior warning, public place to be communicated no more than one hour before, no bodyguards, no tricks, no photography, no more tailing McBride or Sylvia.

They finished and moved their restless party toward the door. Brown told Angus to settle the bill, which he did in hundred-dollar bills.

•   •   •   •

They all walked out together to find that Sylvia's Prius had been towed.

Brown offered to give Sylvia a lift home.

"Thanks, I'll ride with McBee."

The Suburban came around the corner and stopped in the street in front of them. Angus stepped forward and opened the back door for his boss.

"Well, let me give you both a lift back to your car then," Brown said.

"Good," McBride said. "That'll give your man here a chance to remove the beep." He thumbed in Joyce's direction.

"The what?"

"The tracking device."

A grin crept across Brown's mouth. He looked at Joyce. "Mike?"

Joyce shrugged. Whatever.

They all piled into the back of the Suburban, except Cora, who climbed into the front passenger side.

"Also," Brown said to Sylvia, "I insist on paying your parking fine. How much do you think it will be? Will $500 be enough?"

"Thank you," Sylvia said.

"Why not a thousand?" McBride said.

"Is it that much?" Brown said.

"Time and trouble."

Joyce shook his head. "Don't be a prick. Five is more than generous."

Angus produced five more bills from his capacious jacket pocket.

One thing was clear: alcoholophilia ran in the Gray-Brown family. The Suburban was equipped with a miniature wet bar. Brown told Angus to open yet another bottle of champagne. He tore the cork out with his teeth.

Cora must have been giving their driver directions. They worked their way through the maze of South Boston traffic and overpasses back around to the far side of the Summer Street overpass and stopped in the street, blinkers on, beside the Office. Everyone in the back got out again.

They stood on the sidewalk with their champagne glasses while Joyce squatted down behind the Office and felt under the bumper. Brown, restless on the street, shifted his weight back and forth on his heels. Joyce stood up again, a cigarette-pack-size transmitter in his hand, showed it to McBride like he was waving a police badge.

"Did you bug my house too?" McBride said.

Joyce pocketed the transmitter. "No."

"Why not?"

Joyce ignored him and waited for Brown to end the meeting.

McBride turned to Brown too: "If I get the feeling anybody is tailing me again, the deal is off."

"I understand." Brown shook his hand and Sylvia's, and said goodbye.

Angus collected McBride and Sylvia's flutes. The Brown party piled back into the big black Suburban and drove off. The driver signaled before changing lanes. Not so much as a parking ticket on Brown.

Data point.

Part Two. Brown.

CHAPTER 33

RETREAT

"First impressions?" McBride said.

"Can be deceiving," Sylvia said. "But not in this case. He's a creep."

"More than the other one?" He opened the door for her.

"Now can you take me to get my car out of tow?"

"Now don't be pissy, Syl."

Mock chagrin: "But it'll be on my permanent record!"

"Well, I guess your dreams of becoming a high end parking valet end here."

He shut the door and walked around and got in the driver's side. "Anyway you made five-hundred bucks on the deal."

"Less the fine, of course, and your half, and my pain and suffering."

He pulled away, heading east on Summer. "No you should keep it. Pain and suffering and all."

"Fiddy-fiddy down the line. I insist."

He took a right at the Westin and headed to the Boston Tow Lot where he parked in front of the main entrance and took the flashlight from the console and got out and slung himself under the front bumper of the Office.

"What are you doing?"

"Checking for the real beep."

"You think the one Joyce showed you was just a decoy?"

"Or maybe there's two. Maybe not. But these fuckers aren't amateurs."

He ran his hands along the underside of the front bumper, then worked his way clockwise around the vehicle, bending down by each of the wheel wells and searching inside the fenders.

Sylvia followed him along, duckwalking. "So what did you think?"

"Of Brown and company?" he said, from under the right front tire. "I don't trust him as far as I could throw his bodyguard. What did you think?"

She squatted down beside him. "What's the deal with the colorful names? Is there going to be another brother named Joe Black? Maybe it's like a crime brotherhood. The Sextuplet Syndicate. And they all have color-coded cover names. That's why they're looking for each other. They're killing one another off. I can't wait to see who has to be Mr. Pink."

McBride gave her a grim look. "You're funny. I don't know, maybe Brown really is their real name. Maybe Morris thinks calling himself 'Gray' is cute."

"But you don't think so?"

"No. I think they're both full of shit."

"You're not so bad yourself."

"How's that?"

"You told him you met his brother three weeks ago. Has it even been a week yet?"

"An investigator could use a date like that to try to isolate when Gray arrived in town, figuring he's staying in a hotel. I gave him a time frame that was believable but wrong."

"Clever."

"The point of the question game is to learn more than you reveal. Use the bait of falsehood to take the carp of truth. That's Shakespeare."

"Was he a dick too, or was that Marlowe? Did we win?"

"Not sure yet. We held our own. We have at least two legit names to work with: Mike Joyce and the attorney, what's his name?"

"Murray Alper. Esquire. Office on Beacon Street."

"That will help us triangulate Johnny Brown."

"But Brown has both our names too."

"Our names won't lead him to our client though. My guess is that there is a long-standing relationship between Brownie and Alper and Joyce. That'll leave tracks."

"And Cora Lobb."

"Probably no help there. My guess is she's just Joyce's little helper slash squeeze."

"Now don't be bitter, loverboy. I'm sure she's doing her best."

"It was too easy to blow her cover. Hell, she didn't really have a cover."

"So she lost your respect because she's a lousy liar? I hope you never refer to me as your little helper slash squeeze."

He looked up from under the rear bumper at her. "I would never call you anything slash squeeze."

She punched him in the thigh and retreated to another topic: "So what are you going to tell Gray?"

"Ow. I haven't decided yet. Depends what we can find out about Brown today." McBride concluded his search with the left front wheel well, finding nothing. "It's probably clean," he said, getting up. "Let's get your silly ass car out of stir, withdraw to my place, put some coffee on, and start the digging."

. . .

They continued their debrief on speaker driving separately home.

"You didn't have much to say at lunch," McBride said.

"I was busy providing moral support."

"I thought he was less creepy than Gray."

"They're both afraid of something," Sylvia said. "But not the same thing, not in the same way. Brown is scared. Gray is dreading."

"Brown is cooler than Gray though. I wouldn't bet on Gray against him."

"We're not giving Gray up to him."

"Not if we don't have to."

"I mean it, McBee."

"Did you catch the way Brownie asked me if I had told our client whether I had identified him yet? Not whether I'd found him, or contacted him, but whether I'd 'identified' him. A man doesn't need to *identify* the brother he grew up with, he wants to *find* him."

"What do you think it means?"

"And the way Brown kept referring to our client as 'he,' not 'my brother,' or 'Sam.' It didn't feel very Philadelphian."

"But obviously they are brothers."

"So were Jacob and Esau."

CHAPTER 34

THE POWER OF THE GREAT

They spent the afternoon at the little table in McBride's living room, hunched over back-to-back laptops. They didn't come up with much, and nothing at all more than ten years old. There was verifiable documentation on Brown's lawyer, Murray Alper: court records, legal records, financial records, school records, and so on, but there wasn't the range of material you'd expect to find for a lawyer with a public practice. They tried calling Alper from a burner on every number they could find, but the lines were either delisted or went unanswered — not even to voicemail. It looked like Alper had never had but one client, and that client — despite his affection for wine, women, wealth, and hockey — had led a remarkably unremarkable life.

"Consigliere," McBride said. "Seriously, mafia dons in WITSEC leave more tracks than our Charlie Brown."

There was background on Mike Joyce too. Former Baltimore narcotics detective. Before that, ten years as a military intelligence officer. But not much to know about him since he came to Boston. Like Alper, he seemed to stay pretty safely inside Brown's pocket.

On Brown himself there was almost no documentary evidence of his existence. Or so it seemed for a while, until Sylvia suddenly slapped the table and said, "I got him! John Fucking Brown. Born Torrington, Connecticut. Led a failed slave uprising in Virginia. Captured and hanged, 1859. It's right here in Wikipedia!"

"You're funny."

"You don't think it's him?"

"Not likely. That John Brown had scruples. I don't think our man does."

"That must be what they hanged him for."

"Now, Justice moves in mysterious ways its wonders to perform. Don't you believe in the rule of law?"

Sylvia's expression suddenly became grim. She sat back and gave McBride a long and solemn look across the table. "You ask me that?" she said, and there was a quaver in her voice.

McBride felt uneasy. "I know," he mumbled, almost inaudibly.

"I believe in the iron law of karma," she said. "I believe in motherfucking justice for all."

Whenever he thought of the night that she had taken justice it made him feel a little sick.

"I know," he said. "I know."

CHAPTER 35

PROGRESS

McBride and Sylvia knocked on door 808 at 0200 sharp — after the usual precautions getting there: this time taking the T to Cambridge, then cabbing back to Boylston, before promenading arm in arm through the Four Seasons and around the Garden.

It took Gray nearly a minute to answer. He looked sleepy in bare feet and a frumpy silver satin dressing gown. Once they were inside he gathered Sylvia in his arms and held her hard against him for quite a while.

While this was going on McBride threw his jacket onto the sofa and sat down in one of the chairs. Still alone, he said, "So what's a man have to do to get a martini around here?"

Gray released Sylvia, saying, "It's so good to see you again."

She gave McBride an embarrassed glance.

"I didn't know if you'd come back," Gray said.

"Why wouldn't I come back?" Sylvia said.

"The wife and all," McBride explained.

"Yes," Gray said, turning away. "I'm sorry." One hand lagging as long as possible on her elbow, he shuffled away to the bar and started making drinks.

Sylvia took the chair next to McBride, hating him with her eyes.

"Were you asleep?" McBride said.

"No," Gray said. "Yes. I nodded off watching television, waiting for you."

"Did you go out today?"

"No."

In a moment he turned and brought forth three beautiful martinis on the lacquer tray. McBride was becoming fond of that tray with its blue running horses design.

Sylvia took one.

McBride took his, and, watching Gray's face, said, "We met your brother today, Morris."

Gray's right hand was just about to close on the last martini glass on the tray when his mind processed what McBride had said —his right hand collided with the glass without closing on it while his left lost its grip on the tray altogether. Glass and tray fell together to the floor. Alcohol and olives splashed over McBride's boots. Gray stood limply gaping down at McBride, all the air gone out of him, a hectic shadow falling over his eyes.

"Dammit," McBride said, trying to get up, but Gray was in his way. "Sit down, Morris."

Gray stepped stiffly backwards.

McBride got up and went to the bar for a towel.

Gray remained as helpless as a statue in the middle of the room.

"Sit down, Morris," Sylvia said, her eyes suddenly glassy.

Gray seemed to feel his way to the little sofa.

McBride sat down in his chair and dabbed at his boots and the carpet with the towel.

"What do you mean?" Gray said. "What do you mean you 'met' him?"

"We had lunch together," McBride said. "In Seaport."

"Oh no," Gray said. "Oh no. Oh no."

"What's wrong, Morris?" McBride said in a hard voice. "You look like you just found your pet hamster in the microwave."

"Would you shut the fuck up?" Sylvia said. She put her glass aside and went to sit with Morris on the sofa. She took one of his hands in both of hers. "What's wrong?"

Gray recovered slightly, looked from her to McBride. "I told you, I told you when I hired you, not to approach him if you found him."

"I didn't approach him. He approached me."

"What? How?"

"My guess is I must have rattled the right cage. Somebody gave him the word that I was showing his picture around town. He hired a pair of his own supersleuths to find out what we were up to. When they realized I had made them, he decided to get formally acquainted. We had an interesting lunch at the Blue Light. He wants me to set up a meet with you."

As McBride talked, Gray's expression progressed from despair to panic. McBride saw Gray's hand, cradled in Sylvia's, harden into a claw.

"What's the matter, Morris? This is progress. You seem less than thrilled."

"You idiot," Gray said. "Why couldn't you do what I asked?"

"Shit happens, chief. Sometimes twice in a day."

"What's his name?" Gray said, his voice hollow, the way you'd ask about a man you'd watched jump off a hotel roof a minute ago.

"He says *your* first name is really Sammy, short for Salmon."

As expected, Gray didn't react to that like it was a disclosure.

"What did he say his real name is?"

"John, short for Johnny."

Sylvia had been leaning away from Gray as he hardened. She let go of his hand and sat back a little, watching him.

For his part Gray contrived to be lost in consideration of developments, avoiding either of their looks. "I need you to tell me," he said, "exactly what you told him about me."

"Well, of course I told him you missed him very much and that you wanted nothing more in life than to be reunited with him."

Gray neither smiled nor frowned. "This is important, McBride."

McBride decided not to waste breath asking why. "I didn't tell him anything. I've already told you more about him than he knows about you."

"If he finds me, he'll kill me."

"You boys really take sibling rivalry to the limit, don't you?"

"How is the meeting to be arranged?"

"He says you're insane. You know who he is, and this whole cat-and-mouse game of yours is proof. I am inclined to believe him." Not really. Tactics.

"No, you're not. You're just baiting me."

"I'm trying to decide whether even another drink makes it worth sitting here any longer."

"I will be happy to make you another in exchange for the information I hired you to provide to me."

"Question. If you think your brother wants to kill you, why are you trying to find him? Why don't you just stay disappeared, or hire protection? How do I know *you're* not planning to kill *him?* How do I know you're not using me to set him up for it?"

"How can I convince you?"

"Honesty is the best policy."

"Tell me how the meeting is to be arranged."

"Sometime tomorrow I will call you both and tell you where to be within the hour. The time and place are up to me. No prior notice, no entourage, no tricks. He's just as paranoid as you are. You should both seek treatment. Maybe go to family counseling together."

"And if I don't agree to meet?"

"Nothing."

"You'll call him and tell him?"

"Maybe. Or maybe I'll just go home and take a nap. For a week."

"Whose side are you on now, McBride? I need to know."

"I always pick the upside. And in family squabbles there isn't one."

"Is he paying you? Did he offer you more money?"

"No."

"Well, I am paying you. To obtain certain information. I want to know his name, his phone number, his address, and everything else you have. You are obligated to turn over to me what I paid you for. Don't you have professional ethics?"

"Some people have ethics. Detectives not so much."

"I could sue you. You could lose your license."

"I hope you kept your receipts."

"I don't understand. Why won't you tell me who he is?"

"Do you want me to arrange the meet or not, Morris?"

Gray glared at him. Fear and hatred. But not for McBride. "All right."

"Super. Now if you'll just slip me the grand you owe me for today, we'll be on our merry way. Or at least I will. I will expect the finder's bonus tomorrow at the meet. Square?"

CHAPTER 36

DARKENING OF THE LIGHT

Sylvia left with McBride. She started talking the second the elevator closed, headed down to the lobby. "What the hell just happened?"

"Did you notice a draft on the loveseat?"

"You know, fuck you, McBee."

"Our sad little lump of dough set up quite hard, didn't he?"

"He's terrified."

"Think he's been playing you?"

"I really hate you now."

They sashayed out past the sleepy desk clerk and into the street. He wrapped his arm around her waist and kept her close. He felt her body stiffening against him, but he held on and she tolerated it.

"I think we'll have to call this one 'The Case of the Drab-Colored Twins,'" he said, whispering now.

"Are you really going to do the meetup?"

"Or how about 'The Case of the Bullshit Brothers'?"

"McBride."

"Yes, Sylly, I'm going to set it up. If only to see whether either of them shows."

"How can you be sure it's not a trap?"

"Oh I'm sure it *is* a trap. A double trap. They're both trying to trap the other."

"You know this?"

"Not only that, they both *know* they're both trying to trap the other. That's what Gray was calculating beside you on the loveseat. That's what he's always been calculating. That's what the other brother was working on at lunch today."

"This is fucking nuts. Why?"

"That's the part of the game I can't figure. We're the pawns on the board. We can watch the other pieces moving, but we're not privy to the purpose."

"So why not walk away?"

"Two reasons. One, I was promised a fat stack if I bring the other king to check. Two, they're not going to let me leave the board. They're each desperately trying to find the other, and I'm the only one who knows them both."

"And me."

"And you."

"Are we in danger?"

"I might be. I pity the fool who takes a run at you though."

"All right, what's the plan?"

"Play our parts out. Pretend to be the tools they take us for."

CHAPTER 37

THE CLAN

Fanned by a cold wind cold daylight brightly burned around the house. The wind rattled at the old glass and sliced in through the uncaulked chinks. McBride finally roused around noon, shivering.

The toilet seat was like an ice block.

He texted Sylvia: — *you up*

She answered in ten seconds: — *no*

— *here or there*

— *got coffee?*

— *no*

— *dunkin*

— *pikc you up in 5*

— *15*

— *10*

— *i still hate you*

— *itll pass*

He could reach the tub faucets from his seat. He opened the hot up all the way to let the water mount up from the basement while he finished his ablutions.

Thirteen minutes later he pulled up in the Office in front of Sylvia's place. She came out dressed for business: overcoat, slacks, heels, blouse. McBride had attired to the same frequency.

It was four minutes to the nearest Dunkin' Donuts. That's how remote, in New England terms, the Spring Pond neighborhood was.

"Call the Brothers Bland, yet?" Sylvia said.

"Need coffee first. Lips numb."

"Verily."

After the first cup, McBride called the number Brown had given him at lunch yesterday.

"Joyce," answered.

"McBride. I was calling Brown."

"What's the plan?"

"Logan airport. Terminal Echo. Tell Brown I'll meet him at the JetBlue desk in one hour. He'll need a ticket and a photo ID to get through TSA. No liquids, gels, lotions, or creams. No firearms, no blades longer than two inches, no—"

"A ticket to where?"

"Anywhere."

"Why Logan?"

"Because I said so."

"I don't like it."

"Even better." McBride clicked him off.

"Who answered?" Sylvia said.

"Joyce. He doesn't like the setup."

"That's probably a good thing."

"That's what *I* said."

"I can take care of him." She seemed be to thinking her attack through already.

"I doubt if that will be necessary. Let's just get this done, get paid, and get out. If everybody just behaves and follows the path of least resistance, there shouldn't be any trouble."

She looked at him. "So we're fucked."

"Basically."

CHAPTER 38

OPPOSITION

Sylvia watched the drop-off area through binoculars from the front seat of the Office on the third deck of the adjacent parking building.

"Joyce and that baby-faced bodyguard just got out of the black Suburban," she reported, her phone on speaker.

McBride was inside the terminal, sitting on a bench seat where he could watch the approaches to the JetBlue ticket desk. He had a *Boston Herald* on his lap and was tapping his foot impatiently. Just another harried business traveler.

"That's it?" he said.

"Yup. Suburban leaving."

"I expect they're casing the setup first."

"Looks like it. They split up. Walking away from each other. Trying to look like they're not scanning."

The two men walked to the opposite ends of the drop-off zone, turned back, and went into the terminal via the nearest respective entrances.

"They're coming inside now," Sylvia said. "Looks like they're working their way back to the middle again. You'll spot them in a second. They're both wearing grey. Joyce is wearing a blazer. The blonde in a sweater. They both have bags."

"That's for show," McBride said. "So do I. — I see Joyce now."

Joyce spotted McBride at the same time and reacted only slightly and continued his survey of the area. Angus the Protector passed by Joyce without speaking. Joyce turned away and went to a ticket kiosk, set his shoulder bag down, put in a credit card, tapped through the screens, and got a ticket out.

"Joyce is fetching a prepaid ticket," McBride said. "Blondie is drifting around like he's waiting for someone."

Joyce came away from the ticketing machine and approached McBride with a small wave like they were salesmen traveling together.

"Joyce is coming over. Stand by." He tapped off.

"Where's your sidekick?" Joyce said, sitting down beside him.

"She called in sick," McBride said. "Where's your lord and master, sport?"

Joyce crossed one knee over the other and affected to people-watch. "One day," he said, to the general environment, "I'm going to indulge myself and let you annoy me."

"Well, you only live once, Mikey. May as well try to enjoy it."

After a minute Joyce uncrossed his legs and picked up his bag as he stood. "Mr. Brown will be here shortly."

"If you chase your horse, the Chinese say…"

Joyce paused and half-turned for the punchline.

"It'll just run away."

Joyce walked away without response.

McBride called: "Be careful out there!"

• • •

McBride called Sylvia back as Joyce walked away and out of the terminal. "Looks like one brother is on board."

"Joyce and the other guy are outside now. Joyce is making a call."

"I expect he's calling the Suburban back to deliver his man."

Indeed, a few minutes later the big black SUV returned and threaded through the narrow drop off lane. Brown got out carrying a black laptop bag, and all three men went back inside the terminal and made their way toward McBride.

McBride met them along the concourse. "Fancy meeting you here, milord!"

Brown was remarkably underdressed for the big occasion: nondescript tan jacket over a faded blue shirt, loose-fit jeans, and worn leather loafers. A black baseball cap embossed with a Bruins puck logo topped it all off.

McBride waved off his escorts. "Just you, Mr. Brown."

Brown smiled large and mirthlessly. "They're just here to see me off."

"Let's go then."

Joyce gave Brown the ticket he'd taken from the kiosk, and McBride and Brown presented their papers to the TSA guard and got into the snaking security queue. Brown was carrying a passport for identification.

"So you do possess ID," McBride said.

"Did someone say I didn't?" Brown was irritable.

McBride asked if he could have a look at it.

Brown said no.

Their progress was slow. Brown was nervous and disinclined to talk. That suited McBride. He passed the time studying the real travelers inching along with them. Straight is the way and narrow the gate. Dreary and drab the endless vacation of paradise.

They unshoed and unbelted and unjacketed and emptied their pockets and lifted their arms inside the scanners, and put themselves back together again on the other side. McBride observed the tub containing Brown's effects: a cheap phone, a very thin leather wallet, a roll of Tums. No keys or coins. His shoes and belt matched, fine brown leather, rich not gaudy.

McBride plucked up Brown's phone before Brown could. "No calls."

Brown started to argue but thought better of it. "So now what?" he said.

"We're meeting at Boston Beerworks. Terminal C."

"C?"

"Yes, C. C for Charlie. C for *Can* you believe your watchers are watching the wrong terminal?"

. . .

It took a few minutes to walk there. Brown scanned the faces and surroundings every step of the way.

The restaurant was busy. They got the last two seats at the bar.

"Where's—?" Brown said.

But stopped when he saw McBride lift his phone.

"Agent Seven, you are a *go* for phase two."

"Uh-huh," Sylvia said. "Does that mean I should call Gray now?"

"Affirmative."

"Wilco. Agent Seven out."

McBride hung up laughing.

"What was that about?" Brown said.

"Just summoning the party of the second part to the family reunion. How about a drink while we wait? You can buy."

"What's your game, McBride? I thought you were going to call us both here at the same time?"

"You're just full of misinformation and misunderstanding. I never said that. I said I would expect you to be where I said to be within an hour of when I said to be there."

"So we're just going to sit around until he arrives?"

"Well I'm going to sit. You can dance if you like."

The bartender pulled up. "What would you like?"

"Do you have a porter on tap?" McBride said.

"Sure."

"Is it handcrafted by fairies in a secret monastery somewhere in Maine?" It was that kind of a joint — everything was handcrafted and artisanal and pure as an angel's ass.

"No," said the bartender without a smile.

"Then I'll drink it."

"Make it two," Brown said with a genuine smile.

"Menus?" said the bartender.

"No thanks," Brown said with the air of a man trying to seize control of a situation that dazzled him.

The bartender nodded and sauntered off.

"Now what's the setup, McBride? Why here of all places?"

"Well, it's an interesting problem, John. How do you arrange a meeting between two people each of whom would like to trick you into leading the other into a trap? Large busy airports are ideal for this kind of job. Very public. No weapons. No good escape routes. Crawling with security. Too many ways in and too much ground to cover for just a couple of lookouts. The cops tend to notice people hanging around outside, and if they happen not to be paying enough attention, your partner can help direct their awareness to any suspicious-looking persons you don't want in the way."

"Well, I won't even bother correcting you, McBride. I understand perfectly why you'd take such a view of the situation. And, if I may say so, *from* that point of view, your solution is ingenious. How long did it take you to come up with it?"

"Eighteen minutes."

"You're an impressive man."

The bartender brought their beers and they toasted.

"Cheers," Brown said.

"Here's to noses lost and brothers found."

"Well now," Brown said, relaxing, "what shall we talk about while we wait?"

*   *   *

"Let's talk about you—" McBride said.

"Boring!"

"You're a remarkably anonymous man, John Brown. We've been backgrounding you since yesterday and we haven't found much. Hardly anything."

"Not much to find."

"For instance, how old are you?"

"Two minutes older than my brother. Or so it was said. I've forgotten the entire incident."

"How long have you lived in Boston?"

"Centuries."

"Ever marry?"

"No. But enough about me. How did you wind up in Boston from China?"

"I came here to lose my religion."

"At Tufts?"

"Your man put together a pretty good jacket on me."

"He's very thorough. That's why he works for me. Is that why you studied philosophy, to help you lose your religion?"

"Or maybe to find a better one."

"And did you?"

"No. Actually I found out that I didn't need a religion."

"Philosophy isn't the typical preparation for a career in police work, is it?"

"The study of philosophy taught me how to reason. And that's great preparation for being a detective."

"You must like Sherlock Holmes stories."

"Holmes is a wonderful character. But as detective stories they're preposterous. The classic Holmes shtick is to glance at some bloke's hat and derive by a series of brilliant inferences his entire life story. But the real world isn't like that. All deductions are really just probabilistic estimations. Suppose there are three links in the chain of inferences that lead you from that smudge on my sleeve to the conclusion that I'm a professional painter. If each inference has even half a chance of being right then you've got at best one chance in eight of coming out anywhere near the truth. You can't send a perp up for twenty on a one-in-eight guess."

"But it's the accumulation of inferences that lead to a correct conclusion. By eliminating the alternatives that do not satisfy all the facts, you zero in on the—"

"Sometimes. In Sherlock's case not usually. And not in the way most people think either. People like to think they're reasoning from facts to a conviction, when they're usually just arranging the facts on hand to support their convictions. Suppose I told you John Doe is a published poet. Would you guess he's more likely to be a truck driver or a professor of literature?"

"Professor," Brown said. "Tell me how I'm wrong."

"In the United States there are about fifty times as many truck drivers as English professors. If English professors are fifty times more likely than truckers to be poets, that means there are about the same number of trucker poets and professor poets. Now suppose you knew your murderer had recently published a lyric in the *New Yorker*, and your two potential suspects are a trucker and a professor. You'd go for the professor, of course. And it's an even bet the real killer walks away clean."

"So who's your favorite truck driver?"

• • •

"T. S. Eliot."

"A telling choice. A very philosophical poet.

> *Footfalls echo in the memory*
> *Down the passage which we did not take*
> *Towards the door we never opened*
> *Into the rose-garden.*"

"And he was hell on wheels in a big rig. Who's yours?"

"Walt Whitman. A sincere and capacious soul."

"He contains multitudes."

The bartender offered them another round of artisanal porters. Brown also ordered a cheese plate "to have something to wash down."

They passed an hour talking philosophy, high and low, while the busy throng of fliers on the move clattered around them. McBride learned nothing else important about Brown, but he wasn't trying very hard either. Now that the case of the brothers Brown and Gray was drawing to its close he was looking forward to getting paid off and having done with the business. He was willing to let Brown keep his secrets. Actually he preferred that he did. Brown was so much like Gray — but better at it, as if he'd had more practice. He had the same large appetites, the roving intelligence, the wary alertness. But the quirks that set McBride's teeth on edge with respect to Gray were moderated in Brown by his self-assurance and self-acceptance. He was perhaps as Gray must be inside the mummy wrappings of his terror. Though both men were haunted by something they shared: Gray was surely being consumed by it, whereas Brown was merely careful of it.

Then Sylvia called back.

"I don't think Gray is going to show."

McBride left the counter and stood by the window where Brown couldn't overhear. Outside on the mirror-bright tarmac, ground crews swarmed and nibbled at the swollen bellies of beached jets.

"But you spoke to him?"

"Over an hour ago. I've been trying to call him back for the last ten minutes, but he's not picking up."

"How did he sound when you talked to him?"

"Tense."

"Did he say he was coming?"

"He didn't say he wasn't."

"What did he say exactly?"

"He said, 'All right, thank you,' and hung up."

"Call the hotel and ring the room."

"I already did that. No answer."

"Are you calling on your own cell or the special bat phone?"

"I've tried both. You want to give it a shot?"

. . .

McBride hung up and called the last number he had for Gray. It could be any one of his burners. No one answered. He called Sylvia back:

"Nada. We should have picked his ass up and brought him here. Go get the Office and meet me up at the curb. I'm coming out."

He went back to the bar but didn't sit down. He fished Brown's phone from his pocket and slapped it down on the bar. "Thanks for the drinks. Looks like the reunion is off."

"What?" Brown's reaction was sharp. It wasn't panic, but it was more than disappointment.

"The other party is a no-show. We're done. Bye." McBride stalked away.

Brown threw a hundred-dollar bill on the bar, grabbed his phone, and ran after McBride. "Where are you going?"

"Home."

"Just like that?"

"Just like that."

"How do you know he's not coming?"

"I know he's not here and I know he's not answering his phone. Maybe he will show eventually. I've lost interest."

They were walking fast through the concourse. Brown caught his elbow, trying to slow him down. "Hold on, McBride."

McBride snapped his arm loose without breaking stride. "I'm done."

But Brown stayed with him all the way outside. "Look, let's work something out. I need your help."

McBride stopped responding.

Sylvia pulled up in the Office and got out and came around to the passenger's side. She glanced at Brown without speaking. McBride took the wheel and drove off like a wagonful of devils.

CHAPTER 39

OBSTRUCTION

He slammed to a stop in the street in front of the mighty Taj and jumped out, barking "Park it," over his shoulder to Sylvia. It was the first thing he'd said since the airport.

He went straight to 808 and found the door open and the maid inside stripping the bed. She jumped when he shot in.

He pretended surprise. "Oh, hello! Sorry! I was just trying to catch old Morrie before I have to head to the airport. Did you see him go out?"

"No, sir."

"Didn't check out, did he?"

"No, sir, not that I know of."

He looked around.

"Damn. Sorry I missed him. I'll just leave him a note. Don't let me get in your way."

He went to the desk and pretended to scribble a note on the hotel stationery.

The maid looked up uncertainly. "Can I help you?"

He ducked around the corner into the alcove next to the bathroom and opened the closet. It was full of clothes, some on hangers, some dropped on the floor. A bag of phones was there on the floor as well. And the poker kit. And beside it the room safe stood open. And empty.

"Fucker," he said to the miniature abyss.

"Can I *help* you?" the maid said again.

He looked at her, ignored her, turned away, and stalked out of the room on knives.

CHAPTER 40

DELIVERANCE

Sylvia was sitting in the Office next to a fire hydrant around the corner. When she saw McBride's face she looked frightened.

McBride jumped in behind the wheel, slammed his door, and roared off.

"What's wrong?" she said. "What's happened?"

"He's gone. Vacated the premises. Left his shit, took his cash, and blew."

"You sure?"

"Son of a bitch owes me a hundred fucking grand!"

"Oh."

"If I wasn't so fucking sick of the pair of them it might be worth hunting him down just to beat it out of him."

He ranted in a similar vein most of the way home.

At a lull in the storm, Sylvia said, "So how did it go with Brown at Logan? Learn anything?"

"It went fine. I drank three pints of beer and talked shit about Sherlock Holmes for an hour."

"So you didn't learn anything?"

"I'm not trying to learn anything. I'm done with the Bobbsey twins."

"Actually the Bobbseys were fraternal. And there were two sets. Nan and Bert, and Freddie and Flossie. I was a big fan."

"OK, they're conjoins. Joined at the fuckwit. Flopsy and Mopsy, the Fuckwits of Siam."

"Wait, that's Beatrix Potter. They're rabbits."

"And the cow jumped over the moon."

She threw up her hands dramatically. "Fine. So what's the plan? Are you really going to let Morris get away without paying you?"

"I'm going to go home and take the boat out. Then I'm going to take a nap. Then I'm going to order some takeout. Then I'm going to read a book. And tomorrow I'm going to wake up from this aggravation like it never happened. May the good Lord keep me ever after free from fuckwits."

"I'm worried about him. Why do you think he would take off like that? Leave all his stuff behind?"

"First, he's crazy. Second, he's nuts. Third, he's wacked in the head."

"There's no talking to you now."

"Yes, that's probably a good plan."

CHAPTER 41

DECREASE

Sylvia knocked on the front door a few hours later and let herself in.

"Hello!" she called. "Guess who!"

"I'm out back!" McBride yelled. He was relaxing with a beer in one of the Adirondack chairs on the porch.

She came through the foyer and out the back.

"Grab yourself a beer," he said.

She returned a moment later with a black bottle of Guinness which she clinked against his as she passed and sat down in the other chair and put her long legs up on the rail. She was wearing a shapeless grey sweatshirt over black running tights.

"I was in the neighborhood," she said.

McBride was in his usual simple style: tattered jeans and worn flannel shirt. "Running?"

"Yup. Need to burn off some of the rich food I've been eating lately. Speaking of rich food, want to order a pizza or something?"

"Sure. Whatever you want."

She started looking up Fauci's on her phone. "Do any sculling this afternoon?"

"Yes. Needed to burn off some of the bullshit I've been eating."

"Feel better?"

"A little."

She called and ordered a large veggie special.

They sat quietly for a while as the twilight faded and the sheen on the water below the yard silvered over and the sky took on the electrical pallor of modern civilization. Lights came on in windows around the lake, and from the trees on the far shore a family of crows squabbled. A bullfrog bellowed from further off. And behind it all the monotonous drone of traffic.

It was well dark when Sylvia broke the silence: "It's getting cold."

"Let's go in."

The pizza delivery arrived just as they entered the foyer. McBride paid the bill and brought it into the living room/kitchen. Sylvia had opened two more beers. They settled on the sofa with their plates and bottles in hand. Sylvia pushed off her running shoes and sat sideways against the armrest, facing him, her legs folded up. He stretched his legs out over the coffee table.

Sylvia said, "I've never seen a case get to you like this one has."

"Sure, you have."

"No, I've seen you get angry about a case, and I've seen you get overly invested in a case, and I've even seen you fall hard for a sexy client, but I've never seen you let a case get under your skin like this one has."

McBride mulled it over, frowning, but didn't reply.

"You know what I think it is?" she said. "You're a bad loser."

"What did I lose?"

"You lost the war against the riddle. The shining knight sallies forth, honor bound to battle the dragon what's destroying the kingdom of truth. — I bet you're not sleeping, are you?"

"You make me sound ridiculous."

She shook her head as she pulled the band from the ponytail of her dark hair. "No. Actually, it's kind of marvelous." She rolled her eyes self-consciously. "You aren't exactly the sort of person you pretend to be, you know. Sure you like to dress yourself up in your cynicism — it's like your armor — but everybody feels the white heat of your intensity anyway. It's almost frightening. You know you intimidated the hell out of Morris."

McBride felt exposed and embarrassed, but he also liked to hear her talk about him — and it furthered his discomfort that he liked it.

"I know you don't like him," she continued after a moment, "and I get that. He is the most peculiar person. But he had a lot of respect for you. I think he even felt guilty about not telling you what it was really all about."

"And what was it all about?"

"I don't know either! But I think he wanted to tell us. I think he was dying to tell someone. But he was convinced he couldn't do it. He honestly believed it was dangerous."

"You know that's psychotic."

"Unless he was right."

"Come on."

"I'm telling you, McBee, there's something going on here that we don't understand."

"Going on between the two of them?"

"Yes. Partly that. And more."

"How do you know?"

"I'd be tempted to say it was woman's intuition if I wasn't such a badass."

"Your ass isn't that bad."

There was a dangerous moment of silence. McBride instinctively started calculating escape routes.

Then Sylvia burst out laughing. "You should see the look on your face!" she shouted. Then she choked and coughed. "Christ, I just snorted half my beer!"

"Sorry, Syl. I forgot to set the safety on my mouth."

"Just get me another beer, bitch!" she cried, still laughing and choking.

He did as instructed. The ancient undersized cinnamon-red refrigerator was just in the corner of the room behind her, but he took the long way around his end of the couch and through the kitchen area to get to it, in case she needed to retaliate. But she was too busy mopping the spit off her chin and chest.

"So anyway," he said, putting his legs back up on the table.

"So anyway. If I didn't know you better, I'd say you've been acting a little jealous lately."

"Sleeping with clients is so unethical!" His tone was mocking.

"Morris was your client, not mine."

"Sophist."

"Hypocrite."

"Cora wasn't a client."

"I wasn't thinking of her, but—"

"Sure you were."

Sylvia smiled and put her empty plate aside on the counter behind the couch. "OK, maybe we've both been behaving badly. But you admit you were jealous?"

"I take the fifth. What about you?"

"I have to pee." She got up.

"Strategy of avoidance."

"I have to pee!" She headed out to the foyer and upstairs in her bare feet. "It's cold as piss in here, McBee!" she called as she went up. "How about doing a fire?"

So he threw some kindling and magazines into the fireplace and lit it with a long-nosed lighter. The inked paper blazed up green and gold and blue.

The kindling was starting to catch when she came back down.

"You were gone long enough," he said.

"Miss me?" Before he could answer she said, "Another round?" and flung open the cinnamon door.

"Are we getting drunk?"

"You always say you can't get drunk on Guinness."

"I say lots of things."

He was feeling goofy. Sylvia was in high spirits after the excitement of the airport surveillance and that cleared away some of the lingering fumes of The Brothers Weird.

Sylvia opened two bottles and let the caps fall on the floor. She handed him his bottle and curled up against the arm of the couch again. It was a small couch, too small to stretch out on. She let her legs down now so her calves were across his thighs. He balanced his beer on her knee.

"Are you really going to let Gray get away?" she said.

"Even if I could track him down, I can't make him pay up."

"I think you could make him an offer he couldn't refuse."

"I'm pretty sure there's a law against that sort of persuasion."

"I don't mean really, but I'm not so sure he wouldn't pay up. I don't think he ran necessarily to cheat you. I think he was scared that his brother might know where he was — that he might follow you back to him, or that you might give him up."

"Do you want me to try to find him?"

"I'm worried about him."

"Explain to me why you care about that flake. What's the attraction?"

"I thought he was sweet. And he was very gentle and kind. And he loved life. I mean really. He was like a kid. He wanted to see everything. And he looked at everything like it was all fresh and new. But he was so paranoid that he could hardly leave the hotel or get out of the limo."

"Boy in a bubble."

"Something like that."

"What about your walk around the Common?"

"He was nervous as hell the whole time. I thought it was me. But it wasn't."

"You're the most unusual person, Syl."

"Yes, I am," she said. "And now I'm hot." She sat up and pulled her sweatshirt off. Under it she was wearing a black running bra — and her swirling tattoos.

The fire spit and hissed as the sap and moisture came out of the green logs.

McBride let the cold beer bottle come down on her bare stomach.

She watched him do it.

"You didn't even flinch," he said.

"Abs of steel."

He traced a loop on her stomach with the heel of the bottle, between the navel-high waist of her tights and the bottom band of her bra. "What is that one? A phoenix?"

"A gryphon," she said without looking. She was watching him, watching how he was looking at her.

Without removing her legs from his lap, she sat up and bent forward and kissed him, and he kissed her back. Her shoulder, where a pink medallion flowered, cupped in his hand, felt cool as satin, and he felt her biceps flex as she lifted her arm and put her hand over his ear and pulled his mouth more fully onto her mouth. He let his hand slip down her back, feeling the lithe bands of muscle above her hips, let it come back up from her hips to the side of her breast under the smooth black bra. She took hold of his chin in her hand and turned his head and started kissing his neck and his ear. He listened to her breath deepen as she turned on, felt the warm wind of it on his neck, wet and smelling of beer.

He had never kissed her, or held her like this, but now without warning he had her in his arms and he felt his heart thudding like a teenager's his first time to second base.

But then three loud knocks struck from the front door.

CHAPTER 42

INCREASE

"What the fuck!" he said under his breath.

Sylvia giggled.

The spell was broken.

The knocks were repeated.

She swung her legs off his lap and he pushed himself up and went out to the foyer. He pulled his shirttail out en route to cover the increase in his pants.

For a second he took the woman standing on the doorstep for a cop in dress blues, then he realized it was a getup.

She was a busty blue-eyed blonde. The badge on her cap looked like it was made of 24-carat plastic. She flashed a fake cred at him. "Is your name Christian McBride?" she said, trying to hold her pretty face hard.

"Who the hell—"

"You are *not* under arrest!" she snapped back. "You do *not* have the right to remain silent. *Nothing* you say will be used against you. You *do* have the right to an escort. If you cannot afford an escort, one will be provided for you. Knowing these rights, are you willing cordially to attend a bodacious party at the home of Mr. John Brown, esquire?"

A black stretch limo was parked in front of the house and a uniformed chauffeur was watching from beside it.

McBride was speechless for a long moment.

Sylvia came into the foyer behind him. She had put her sweatshirt back on. She was laughing.

"Miss Sylvia, I presume?" said the fake cop, the slightest twinge of humor appearing in one corner of her mouth. "Mr. Brown would be pleased if you also would attend the festivities." She nodded curtly.

"What's the occasion?" Sylvia said.

"Mr. Brown would like to express to you both in person his appreciation for the care and consideration you have extended in his affairs and to make amends for the trouble and discomfort connected thereto." She delivered herself of these prepared speeches with impressive glibness, but the affair at the airport had only been a few hours ago.

"What, now?" McBride said.

"Yes, sir, Mr. McBride. Mr. Brown invites you and Miss Sylvia to make use of his car and driver, and I am ready to assist you in any way."

McBride turned and looked at Sylvia. The conversation that took place in silence between them lasted about three seconds:

— What the hell just happened?

— It's too absurd to go back to the couch now.

— Well, fuck it, let's go to the party then.

Then Sylvia said, aloud, "I need to get cleaned up."

McBride turned to the messenger. "Could you take her around to her place to change, then come back for me?"

"Very good, sir!" said the fake cop.

CHAPTER 43

BREAKTHROUGH

The limo returned half an hour later. McBride was watching at the door and went out. The fake cop got out from the front and opened the wide back door for him. Sylvia was waiting inside with a bucket of champagne. McBride had gone to the trouble of putting a blazer on over his flannel shirt, blue jeans, and hiking boots, but Sylvia had showered and tied her hair back in a loose ribbon and changed into a peach jacket over a knit white dress and white heels. He got in and sat beside her on the back bench, and tried not to look at her because it made him uneasy. The fake cop poured a second glass of champagne and gave it to him, then shut them in and got in up front beside the driver.

"What the hell are we doing?" McBride said.

She dodged the question. "Going to a party."

He let her dodge it.

"She was going to be your court-appointed escort," Sylvia said, nodding toward the fake cop. "Her name is Liz. In case you need to know later."

He gave her a look.

So the question was settled: they were not going to talk about the episode on the couch. For a minute, they quietly studied the bubbles dancing in the fancy crystal flutes between their knees.

"I know I drink too much anyway," McBride said, fingering his glass, "but the brothers, Jesus…"

Sylvia took a drink and crossed her legs and let her shoe dangle from her toes. "You know, this case isn't over yet, McBee."

"It is until I see some cash."

She lowered her glass to her knee. "See, that's what I meant about—" She stopped without finishing, letting him leave his armor on.

So they wouldn't refer to the discussion that led up to the episode either.

"We should have a plan for tonight," he said.

"OK, how's this: I'll distract him with my charms, you rob him blind."

He laughed grimly. "That'll work."

CHAPTER 44

COMING TO MEET

Fake cop Liz opened the limo door with a smile and said, "Welcome to Andromeda."

Andromeda was not your typical New England manse. It looked like it had been carried over from the Baltic coast and jumbled in the reassembly: a rambling grey and white brick chateau with art nouveau flourishes. A wide colonnade porch fronted the drive. Liz led them through to the main door, a massy slab of pine planks. It opened into a bright white-marbled foyer that extended at least as far as Vermont. Happy party chatter sluiced into it from all directions. Someone was playing a piano to a sing-along. Elsewhere men were shouting at a hockey game on television. And John Brown, radiantly attired in blue silk tunic and trousers, was walking quickly in bare feet up the centerline of the foyer, hefting a big smile.

"I'm so glad you came," he said, spreading his arms to display himself. "Look I wore these just for you." He collapsed his display into a vast embrace for Sylvia. "You look marvelous, Miss — may I call you Sylvia? You look marvelous."

"Thanks." Her smile was a little more than polite, but a little less than friendly.

Brown turned to McBride and shook his hand warmly in both of his own.

"And you look — Well…" He surveyed him theatrically. "Like a man who prefers to get to the point."

"You know nobody dresses like that in China anymore?"

Brown feigned shock. "What, no blue?"

McBride laughed. Brown shared Gray's dramatic flair, but his timing was better. On the other hand his act was stagier. He was nervous.

"Thank you, Liz, for fetching our guests of honor. You can run along now. Take the rest of the night off. Maybe go arrest some dogsbody."

"Any dogsbody in particular?" she said, but didn't wait for a reply. She took her cap off as she walked away and tossed it like a frisbee through a dark doorway. The cap triggered a motion-activated light inside, revealing an open coatroom with more apparel on the floor than on hangers.

Brown turned a different way and indicated they should follow him. "I don't believe in giving tours," he said. "I think it's a lot more fun for you to explore on your own. Make yourself at home. However, I need to introduce you to George."

He led them past a fountain — a copper Centaur — in the midst of the foyer, past the foot of a broad curving stair, through a short alcove under the stair, into a well-lit oak-panelled office, where he spotted through the glass along the back wall a woman in jeans and T-shirt lugging a bundle of linen along the serviceway. He called after her, "Hey, where's the Maestro, darling? — Send him in here please."

Another wall of the room was lined with a bank of security monitors set in ornate plaster frames like they were old paintings. Each one showed a different view of the house or the grounds.

A thin solemn-faced middle-aged man in a conservative suit that looked worked in came quickly along the aisle outside the glass and ducked into the office.

"George, what the fuck," Brown said.

The Maestro didn't exactly snap to attention but his attention focused down real quick, and he didn't look like a person whose attention wandered much anyway.

"Nobody's on watch?"

"Tiny Jones is on tonight," the Maestro said, and, moving only his eyes, confirmed that Tiny was not hiding in plain sight, and then, without prior warning, erupted with a spine-chilling bellow: "*Jones!*"

McBride actually jumped at the sound.

"I'll kick his ass directly, John," the Maestro said. "Probably taking a piss."

"He's on watch. He can either piss in his pants or call for relief."

"Yessir."

"Now I want you to meet two new friends." He gave him their names, and his to them: "This is George Marks. He runs the house for us. — George, put them up near me tonight."

"Are we staying?" McBride said.

"If you want to. I hope you will. We have things to talk about. But if you decide you want to go, let George know, or let someone let George know, and he'll have the car brought up. Otherwise, anything you need, change of clothes, ibuprofen, extra condoms, whatever, he's your man."

"Near you?" said Marks. "In the East room?" His expression conveyed a hint of special favor.

"Perfect," Brown said. Then to them: "Do you two sleep together?"

Caught off guard, neither of them answered quick enough.

"Well, decide later," Brown said with a casual wave.

It was impressive how quickly he read them. That question was no accidental faux pas.

Tiny Jones came in from the serviceway at a trot. Marks turned on him like a terrier on a mouse. Brown ushered his guests back out while Tiny enjoyed the finest dressing down of his young career.

Brown led them across the foyer and through an open set of double glass doors into a capacious anteroom that let into an even bigger reception hall. The anteroom was scattered with round-top white-clothed tables bearing multi-level trays of liquor, wine, and finger foods. A pair of young women in short skirts and long lace stockings were poking several different colors of melon balls into each other's mouths and giggling like idiots. They waved.

Brown saluted back.

"Who are they?" McBride said.

"Foggiest!"

A few dozen clownfish and parrotfish fluttered through a long bright aquarium set in the far wall.

Passing through into the reception hall they found the sing-along group and the piano player along with a couple dozen other people clumped into several little fists of activity: dancing or laughing or just holding each other up. The room was wedge-shaped, the outer wall a curving quarter-circle of floor-to-ceiling paned glass overlooking a pond.

Brown swirled them into the middle of the mix and called not too loudly for attention. Maybe half the occupants complied. The pianist paused.

"Everyone, *these* are the official guests of honor tonight. Miss Sylvia, call her Sylvia, and Mr. McBride, don't call him Christian."

A couple of people came up to get acquainted.

Brown turned to go. "We'll talk later."

"Why not now?" McBride said.

"Can't just now. Relax and have some fun. We've got all night."
He walked away as he spoke, flagging that casual wave of his.

A man dressed in a yellow tracksuit offered to fetch them a drink, saying, "We have *every*thing! *Every*thing. What do you like?"

"I like *every*thing," McBride said.

"Look out, folks!" tracksuit yelled, "there's a *smart*-ass on the premises! — Well come on now, we'll find you something special."

He took Sylvia by the hand and pulled her toward the anteroom. McBride followed, trailed by some new friends.

CHAPTER 45

GATHERING TOGETHER

It was half past one before they saw Brown again. George Marks found them lounging in the library with some newly acquired friends.

"You go ahead," Sylvia said. "Let me know how you make out."

So she stayed behind and Marks led McBride through some narrow corridors and a couple of security doors that were unlocked by a card reader, coming at last to a wide oak-panel door that Marks introduced as "Mr. Brown's private office."

The door opened into one end of a large oval chamber. Unlike the public areas of the house it was colorfully rather than brightly lit. Except for the tall paned glass windows around the far end, and the interruptions of several doorways, the walls were all bookshelves and cabinets below and paintings and sculptures above. The floor was clothed in a massive maroon Persian rug. The slightly domed ceiling was painted with gauzy clouds from which ancestral divinities stood lazy sentinel. At the business end of the room a heavy library table stood under the paned windows, scattered with books and surrounded by eight expensive desk chairs — chairs with web seats and good suspension, chairs for working in. At the near end of the room a quartet of navy-blue leather easy chairs squatted around a puffy gold ottoman that looked something like the winning pumpkin from a 4H contest, memorialized in gold leaf.

It was one of the most beautiful rooms McBride had ever seen.

When they entered, Brown was sitting at the conference table reading a tablet display. He dropped it, smiled large, rose, and came forward quickly.

"Great! Hello, McBride!" He had changed out of the Chinese silks into khakis and a sweater, but his feet were still bare, his steps soundless on the lush rug. McBride got the big two-handed shake again. "Thanks, Maestro," Brown said to Marks. "Now bring us something to drink, will you?"

"I'm already drunk," McBride said.

"I distrust a man who says 'when.' Can you be trusted?"

"I didn't say 'when.' I'm just giving you fair warning, the drunker I get the plainer I speak."

"Better and better. — Bring us something gentle and sweet, George. Something good."

"Sure. I'll see what I can come up with."

"And some popcorn!"

"Of course." Marks ducked out.

"Popcorn?" McBride said.

Brown steered him toward one of the quartet of fat chairs. "It's my only vice," he said. "Well, that, and lying about my vices."

McBride collapsed into a chair. He was even drunker than he had realized.

Brown flopped into the chair to the right and crossed his legs.

"Have you been enjoying yourself?"

"Yes, actually." McBride petted the leather upholstery: it felt like velvet.

"Outstanding."

"They say the party goes on twenty-four seven."

"Three-sixty-five! I like to have people around."

"In Xanadu did Kubla Khan. Must be quite an operation, logistically speaking."

"George is a master. We even have a full-time social coordinator."

A sharp light tap on the office door was followed by Marks, pushing a narrow silver serving cart bearing two small glass bowls of popcorn, two bottles of liquor, and two highball glasses.

"Would you prefer cognac or port?" he said, pulling up behind the couch.

"I think cognac," Brown said.

"For you, sir?"

"What's good for the goose," McBride said.

He poured out two glasses and handed them and the popcorn bowls over. Brown plopped his bowl down atop the chair arm like it wasn't even the flesh of a sacred calf without spot or blemish.

McBride did the same and nipped one kernel into his mouth. It tasted like pure clear sweet crispy butter.

"My god," he said. "It's like angels having sex in my mouth."

Brown laughed and raising his glass said, "Now chase it with the Delamain."

McBride did. It went down like thin honey. He wished he was sober enough to drink the whole bottle.

Marks informed them both that "Miss Sylvia has gone to bed," and stepped out again.

They munched and sipped for a minute or two in blissful silence.

Finally Brown decided it was time to get down to business. "I was afraid you wouldn't come," he said. "Why did you?"

"We were invited."

"Aristotle enumerated the types of causes. That's not the type I meant. What were they again? Material, formal, efficient, and ...?"

"Final."

"Right. I have been thinking about your critique of Sherlock Holmes. Have you ever thought how detective work is a kind of divination?"

"But in a different direction. Past and future." McBride pointed his glass either way.

"Not really. We're all stuck in the present. We look at the past to understand the present. We guess at the future to comfort ourselves here and now. Mystery is our common enemy. Holmes' inductive leaps are entertaining because they satisfy our desire to believe that the world is comprehensible. The more attention we give to the moment, the less mysterious it is."

"But we're still gonna die."

"No! I'm not dead *now*. And the *now* is eternal."

McBride nodded. "Divination as divinity. Mebbe." He pouted. "I'll think about it harder when I'm awake."

Brown grinned, impressed with himself. "Skoal!"

They clinked and drank. Brown poured a second round.

"So what is it, John. What's the pitch?"

"The pitch?"

"Why am I here? Why the red-carpet treatment? I'm not saying you're not a swell guy, and yes, I have had a very pleasant evening here in Shangri-La. However, it's been a very long, very strange, and very annoying day. Was the airport just this afternoon? Christ, feels like a week ago. Anyway, I'm too tired to fence with you. So if that's the only way we can do this thing, then I'm going to have to go to bed and we can dance it out tomorrow — or whenever I wake up again, which might not be for a year or two."

"You know, McBride, you talk more when you're tired. Most people are the other way around."

McBride popped another kernel. Waited.

"All right," Brown said, "the thing is, I need your help."

McBride had been hoping he could finish the cognac before Brown pissed him off too much.

Brown put on a resigned tone, as if there was just no way to say this without being ridiculous: "I want you to help me find my brother. Again."

McBride snorted humorlessly. "Am I your brother's keeper?"

"He's disappeared, hasn't he? That's what happened when he didn't show today, isn't it?"

"I heard he mixed up the directions and went to the wrong terminal. I think he's on a flight to Tahiti. Or was it Fiji?"

"You are literally my only connection to him. You're the only chance I have of locating him."

"Can I ask you a question? Is it like an incest thing with you two? I mean, for fuck sake, let it go."

Brown looked perplexed. "I think he's dangerous."

"Then by all means seek him out. Speaking of living forever in the eternal now. Some people really thrive on danger. Mercenaries. Base jumpers. Have you considered racing cars? That's a nice deadly rich man's hobby."

"I want you to find him to help me protect myself from him."

"Autoerotic asphyxiation. I heard that's a really good way to die."

"Will you help me?"

"It's really not my line, John. I could put you in touch with some people who do that sort of work. They're dependable, good boys."

"Sammy is a violent paranoid psychotic. If you know him, you know that. He needs to be in a hospital. I think he is trying to kill me."

"The answer is no. This cognac, however, is like drinking nectar."

"Do this thing for me and I'll buy you a crate of it."

"See, now you've gone and cheapened what had been a pure and sacramental experience up to now."

"I'm sorry," Brown said. "That was in poor taste. I know you're not a man who can be bought."

"Anybody can be bought. The trick is to offer the right currency." He immediately regretted the implication that Brown might make a better offer.

Brown took it just that way. Leaning forward, with urgency in his voice, he exhorted, "Find him because it's the right thing to do. Because he needs help. Because he's alone in the world. Because it's what you do. Because you want to finish the job. Because the challenge is what you live for."

McBride took another thoughtful sip, waited a beat, pretended to think it over. "You should go into sales. Not that you need the money. But because it's what you do. What you're good at. What you live for." He failed to keep a straight face and started laughing.

Brown laughed too, but only to be polite. "All right, all right. But tell me at least what your objection is to taking my case. Is it me? Because you don't trust me? Because I offended you by having you followed? By the way, that business with Cora wasn't my idea. She works for Mike. I wasn't consulted on that, well, maneuver."

That was enough. McBride set the rest of his drink aside, no longer enjoying it, and stood up, a little unsteadily.

"Thanks for the nightcap, Johnny. I think I'll turn in."

Brown didn't argue. He stood and took McBride by the elbow, sensing how drunk he was. "No, thank *you*. For everything you've done. I'll have George show you to your room. I'm so glad you came. You're welcome to stay as long as you like. Sleep as late as you please. Come down when you wake and George will set you up with breakfast."

Marks opened the office door on cue and took delivery of the guest.

CHAPTER 46

PUSHING UPWARD

Marks led McBride upstairs to a guestroom in another end of the rambling house. McBride puzzled half-consciously over the general shape of the place. Something like an H maybe.

Marks, with his hand on the door handle, whispered, "There are pajamas laid out on the bench at the foot of the bed. If you need anything else, there is a bell button on the nightstand, or come out to the hall and someone will assist you. Good night, Mr. McBride." Marks opened the door for him and let him go in, then closed it soundlessly behind him.

Moonlight filtered through gauzy curtains at the far side of a sea of white carpet. There was a single king-size four-poster bed and Sylvia was gently snoring in it, like the deities on Brown's ceiling a shapely form concealed in cloudy comforters. McBride was too tired and drunk to fool with the pajamas. He sat down on them on the bench and quietly stripped down to his underwear.

It would be a mistake not to hit the head before lying down. He pushed himself up from the bench and stood swaying, his naked feet finding no purchase in the marshmallow carpet. The bathroom seemed leagues away across southern darkness. Briefly, dully, scratching his balls, he weighed the risks of the needful adventure, before finally giving it up. He felt his way around to his side of the bed and slipped in softly under the clouds, careful not to touch Sylvia.

Had he ever had a longer stranger day? Before he could answer, he was out.

CHAPTER 47

OPPRESSION

McBride woke not knowing for a while where he was. Or what day it was. Or whose body he now occupied.

There was a lot of light in the room. Peering out through swollen eyelids he saw knife blades of sun slicing into the room through the louvered blinds on a pair of patio doors. The gauzy curtains were gone and the room was blazing white — much too white — ceiling and walls and carpet — all malevolently white.

The sound of a running shower came from somewhere nearby. Sylvia was not in the bed.

He needed to piss. Badly. His dick was so hard it hurt. The sound of the streaming shower was like being waterboarded with piss. Waiting was not an option.

However, it took him minutes, perhaps hours, to disentangle his form from the creeping vines of comforters and bedsheets and pillows. Everything seemed to catch on his woody.

At last he got one arm free and used it to wrench the rest of his body out. The horrific white sea of carpet was a terrifying distance below the mattress. No ladder in sight, he slid off the edge of the bed like he was dangling off a rooftop and dropped to the floor. He lurched across the pillowy carpet toward the sound of the shower, and quietly let himself into the bathroom. His foggy plan was to slip in, relieve himself, and slip out again undetected.

The open-face shower stall was really just another small room off the main bathroom, undisguised by any curtain or door. Sylvia was standing with her back to the stream, head back, letting the water rain over her face, sable hair hanging straight down between her shoulders like a nun's veil. Her tattoos coiled and danced under the flowing sheets of water. She looked like a beech stump or a wood nymph, standing in a spring shower, graffitied by Michelangelo. For a moment, awestruck, he forgot to look for the toilet. And she saw him, of course — turned her head to look at him like she'd felt his eyes on her.

"What the fuck, McBee," she said, blinking under the water, not covering herself.

If a painting of Pallas Athena had suddenly turned and looked him in the eye he couldn't have been more startled. He jumped so hard he lost his balance.

"I have to piss!" he said, and it came out in a shout.

There was nowhere to hide for either of them. The toilet was in full view of the shower. He stood sideways to it with his back to her and pulled the front of his shorts down, but there was no way to bend his boner down to that angle.

He looked over his shoulder. She was watching him.

"Can you turn around, please?" he yelled.

"Jesus, you're a baby!"

"Just give me a break, will you."

The shower stopped. "I'm done anyway."

He heard her stomp and splash in bare feet out of the shower, felt the breeze of her body pass behind him and out the bathroom door, turned and saw her striding away across the bedroom, slammed the door on the breathtaking vision of her thighs and back. There were twin fish on the cheeks of her ass, curling in opposition, red and blue, yin and yang Pisces.

CHAPTER 48

THE WELL

While they dressed McBride summarized his late-night discussion with Brown.

They had just finished when Marks tapped on the door. "May I come in?"

McBride opened it. "How did you know we were up?"

Marks smiled. "Good morning, Mr. McBride, Miss Conti. Mr. Gray would be pleased if you would join him for brunch."

"You go ahead," Sylvia said.

"No, come on," McBride said. "Don't you need coffee?"

"Maybe just a bucket or two."

"You have coffee, don't you?"

"Wells of it," Marks said.

"Come on. I can't face this morning alone."

"Is it still morning?" Sylvia said.

"Half past twelve," Marks said.

CHAPTER 49

REVOLUTION

Marks took them to a sunny breakfast room sticking out from yet another angle of the second floor. Brown, reading the *Boston Herald*, was seated on the far side of a large round white-linened table within a three-quarters-round grid of colonial-paned windows. He looked like he was sitting in a cage. Below the windows a manicured pond wrapped around this corner of the house. Two blazing white swans cruised like movie props.

"I swear to Christ," McBride said, "this is the whitest fucking house I've ever seen. You should give everybody safety shades. My retinas hurt."

"Good morning, McBride!" Brown said, folding his paper. "Good morning, Sylvia! I do like things bright and cheery. You two look marvelous. Sleep well?"

Marks pulled out a chair for Sylvia on Brown's right. McBride took the only other chair, opposite.

Marks filled their coffee cups. "What would you like to eat?"

"I'm having my favorite breakfast," Brown said. "Caviar, blini, champagne, and coffee." He pointed at the middle of the table with a mother-of-pearl caviar spoon. "And there's strawberries and melon and whatever."

"That works for me," McBride said.

Sylvia asked for a bagel.

Marks dismissed himself.

They made small talk. Brown asked Sylvia if she'd had a good time last night. She had. Marks delivered Sylvia's bagel and left again.

"Good?" Brown said.

"Excellent."

"Quiet this morning," McBride said. "What happened to the never-ending party?"

"Waxes and wanes. Midday tends to be quieter. People have to sleep. And I guess some people have jobs."

"Friends of yours?"

"I'm broad-minded. Speaking of jobs, have you given any thought to my offer?"

"I already—"

"We'll do it," Sylvia said.

"Outstanding!" Brown was bursting with enthusiasm.

McBride looked at Sylvia curiously. "Wait a—"

"I want to find him," Sylvia said. "We might as well get paid to do it."

Brown dropped his hand onto Sylvia's arm on the table. "I had guessed you were the smart one."

She put her hand under the table.

"You're a good team," Brown said.

"We're just friends," she said. "I help him out sometimes."

Brown fiddled with a corner of the newspaper for a minute then looked back at McBride. "I've heard there's a particular connection between the two of you."

"You've heard?" McBride said.

"You were the lead detective when Sylvia's mother was killed," Brown said matter-of-factly. "I remember reading about the case at the time. I read the paper front to back every day. What a terrible thing it was. And how much more terrible for the kidnapper to walk. I can't imagine how anyone—" (glancing at Sylvia) "And then for him to disappear like that." (Back to McBride.) "Not hard to understand why you decided to take early retirement."

A late-season frost fell into the room.

Sylvia leaned forward and studied Brown's expression, which trembled a little under the strain of remaining perfectly placid. "The thing that makes you special, John Brown," she said, "is that you don't have any of the hindrances that hold the rest of us back. We slog our way through life without enough money or brains or audacity. But you have all the money, and all the smarts, and none of the scruples. The one thing you can't control is your brother. And that scares the shit out of you."

Brown's lips quivered between a scowl and a grin a few times before settling on a wry smile. "You like him better than me."

"That's why I want to find him. And I dislike you enough to let you pay us to do it. With the understanding that when we find him, it's up to him to decide what we do next."

Brown looked at McBride. "She's incredible."

"She has her moments."

"Do you agree with her?"

"About you? Plato said that wealth can never make an evil man at peace with himself."

"You think I'm an evil man?" He pretended to be pretending to be hurt.

"I think you're still trying to figure a way to buy invisibility."

Brown became arch now. He had more changes than Coltrane. "I like a man who speaks his mind. Think of it, just forty-eight hours ago we were all getting acquainted at a diner in Fort Point. Twenty-four hours ago we were drinking beer in Terminal C waiting for *him*. And now here you are in my house and you're working for me!"

"You know what you and your double remind me of?" McBride said. "That episode on the original *Star Trek* with the pair of half-black half-white aliens." McBride cut a border down the center of his face. "Chasing each other through eternity. Aside from being polar opposites you're practically identical."

"I remember that one," Brown said pleasantly. "That was a funny one. But let's get started now, shall we? Any guesses where he went? Tell me everything you know about him."

Sylvia said, "No."

They both looked at her in surprise.

"No what?" Brown said, with an undisguised tinge of annoyance.

"We didn't tell him anything about you either," McBride said.

Brown glanced from one to the other. McBride saw how rapidly he calculated. "But he already knows about me. Otherwise why do you think he didn't insist? Why would he disappear without getting from you what he paid you for?"

"Unlike my partner, I don't give a damn about Gr— your alter ego." (He nearly forgot they had not revealed the alter's working title.) "But I do agree with her about getting paid. As long as I'm being well compensated I am willing to continue being a pawn in your battle of wits. For a day or two anyway."

"More knight than pawn, I think."

"It's not a good analogy. Both sides don't play the same piece against each other."

"Double agent?"

"Double. Triple. Mirror, mirror, on the wall, who's the most duplicitous of all?"

"Through the Looking-Glass," Sylvia said.

Brown turned approvingly back to her. "Wheels within wheels. All right, then what are the terms of our arrangement?"

McBride said, "You pay me — *us,* five-hundred apiece a day. We'll find him and arrange for another meeting."

"Is that what *he* paid you?"

"Deal or not?"

"How do I know you're not billing both of us to find the other?"

"Fuck you."

"Ask your man Joyce," Sylvia said.

Brown dropped it. "Even if you find him—"

"We'll find him," Sylvia said.

"Even *when* you find him, why would he agree to a meeting again, or show up for it?"

"I'll make sure he shows," McBride said.

"How?"

"Duplicity."

CHAPTER 50

THE CAULDRON

They set to work immediately after the meal. Brown invited them to stay with him while on the case. McBride said he'd think about it. Brown put a car and driver at their disposal. The driver was the same Teutonic Apollo that had chauffeured them and Fake Cop the night before, but the car was one of Brown's black Suburbans. They talked quietly in the back seat on the way downtown.

"You're scaring our new client," McBride said.

Sylvia checked to see if he was mocking her. He wasn't. "Out of the frying pan into the fire."

"You really care about Morris, don't you?"

"I think we should find him before Brown does."

"We're finding him *for* Brown."

"No, we're not. But you know he's got Joyce looking too."

"True."

"What are we doing today?"

"Jumping into the fire. Have you ever seen that *Star Trek* episode with the black and white aliens?"

"Everybody has seen that."

"John Brown hasn't. There's nothing funny about that one. Why would he lie about it?"

"Why didn't you ask him?"

"He'd just chase it with another lie. Why didn't he just say, I never saw that one?"

"Because everyone has seen it."

"Right. But he doesn't know that, does he? And do you notice his accent is different from Gray's? I can't make out what kind of accent Gray is supposed to have. He's the one that sounds like he grew up kicking around Europe. But Brown sounds like he got off the bus from Ohio about a week ago and is trying to learn to drop his Rs. It's like those bastard Bush brothers. Neither of them picked up daddy's patrician lisp. Little Georgie affects his stupid Texas drawl. Jebbie talks like he's afraid somebody might figure out he's really not from nowhere."

"So do you think they're really politicians or that they didn't really grow up together?"

"Something struck me at lunch two days ago. A couple of things. One was when Brown wanted to know how long we'd been looking for him, how long we'd been working for his brother, he said 'When did he first contact you?' 'He.' Not 'Sam,' or 'Sammy,' or even 'my brother.' 'When did *he* first contact you.' He consistently refers to his sibling like that. There's a psychic distance there that doesn't square with the concerned brother who just wants to see that his twin gets the help he needs."

"So what's it mean?"

"Suppose," McBride speculated, "it's Brown that's the prodigal son, not Gray. Suppose Brown is the one who's been hiding."

"He keeps a pretty high profile."

"But he doesn't have any traceable history. Anybody who knew his real name wouldn't have anything to go on to track him down. Maybe he didn't know Gray was alive until now. Maybe he didn't need to hide from anyone who knew him because he didn't think anyone who knew him was alive."

"How could a person be mistaken about whether everyone in his family was dead?"

"OK it doesn't make sense."

"None of it does." She looked out of the window. I-95 traffic dodging and weaving. "I don't have a good feeling about how this one ends."

CHAPTER 51

THE AROUSING

McBride had the limo take them back to the Taj and let it sit out on the street while they went in and waved Brown's money all over the building, buying information.

Frogface was manning the desk again today. He told them he had not seen Gray leave yesterday, that he had not checked out, that he had not left a forwarding address or any other contact information, that he had paid by the week, always paid in cash, but had not settled his account for the current week, that he had tipped the desk staff handsomely every week, and that he had not returned or been in touch since yesterday after luncheon. He also gave them the name of Gray's barber (who always checked in at the desk before going up).

The maids on eight told them Gray was not neat but not dirty, that he always left a lovely tip, and that he had not said anything prior to leaving. One of them remembered the name of the tailor that Gray liked to have come to the room; his label was in all of Gray's suits.

For lunch they took tea in the French Room — savory finger sandwiches, assorted canapes, and delectable pastries — and learned from the waitstaff that Gray had always tipped handsomely, that he was very fond of cocktails and lemon curd, and that he had not made his usual appearance the day prior. One of the waiters told them that Gray frequently called down to the kitchen at the end of the day for a special treat and that the staff would play rock-paper-scissors for the chance to take it up because there was always a handsome tip and Gray was a lonely eccentric who loved to tell tall tales and make you laugh.

"Like what, for example?" McBride asked.

"One time he told me he was a feral child, that he'd been raised by black bears in the Smokey Mountains in Tennessee. Another time he said he was an android who had been sent to earth on a secret mission by space aliens."

"What was the mission?"

"To save the world from another alien who was going to destroy it."

"You ever get the feeling he was fucking nuts?"

"Nah. Just enjoyed bullshitting. Another time he said he was a professional hockey player. I asked him when was that. He says, I ain't decided yet. It wasn't serious. I seen crazy before. I got a cousin thinks he's married to Charlize Theron. That's crazy. It wasn't like that."

The doormen told them they didn't even know Gray was gone, that they hadn't seen him leave yesterday, that he always tipped handsomely, and that they were sorry to hear he was gone. One of the doormen said he knew the service Gray had hired to chauffeur him and Sylvia a few days ago, and gave them the name.

Next they had Brown's limo follow them while they walked to the bank where Sylvia had gone with Gray to visit his safe-deposit box (two blocks down Arlington). There they got into trouble with the manager for flaunting their bribery money around the place. He seemed shocked to see filthy lucre on display in his tidy bank. McBride goaded him with disdain. The bank manager thundered that no one had seen Mr. Gray in several days and that even if they had they would certainly not be induced by tawdry proffers of cash to say anything about it. So it was that the cheapest chunk of useless information they bought that day came from a professional profiteer.

They spent the rest of the afternoon having Apollo the Charioteer take them around to see the tailor and the barber and the limo service driver who all reported that Gray tipped handsomely, had not been in touch, made a good martini and told a good tale, and so on and such like. Jason the limo driver remembered Sylvia and affected a conspiratorial air which set her teeth on edge.

In the back of Brown's car on the way back to Weston, McBride asked her about it: "What was that about?"

She was slumped back in the seat, dark and exhausted. "I guess it was about sharing the guilt."

"Informing on a client? He didn't even tell us anything."

"I wanted to put my foot through his spleen."

"Now, now. Eyes on the prize. A boy gotta make a buck how he can."

"I hate this job."

"The job or the case?"

"I hate you."

"Water off a duck's back."

CHAPTER 52

MOUNTAIN KEEPING STILL

Brown called McBride on his cell and asked if they'd be joining him for dinner. They had Apollo take them to Peabody first to pick up changes of clothes.

The main drive in front of Andromeda was already lined with cars when they arrived around sunset. They saw, as they passed the main entrance, several new arrivals tumbling up the steps and in through the open door. Marks was waiting at the side entrance for them with another house staffer, who made off with their overnight bags. Marks took them through the security doors to the private wing where they discovered Brown alone in his library looking as though he had meant to be caught working alone, but the space felt only recently solitary.

Sylvia took in the ovaloid room — the maroon rug, the gods gazing down from the welkin — uttering under her breath, "Wow."

Brown rose, a little theatrically, from one end of the work-table and instructed them to make themselves comfortable, please. Marks waved them toward the four fat easy chairs. They all settled in. Brown threw his bare feet up on the ottoman.

Marks went to a small recessed bar and started mixing drinks.

"This is the heart of my little domain," Brown said to Sylvia. "Closed to the public. Strictly off limits. Except for personal friends and business associates."

The entry opened behind them and Mike Joyce admitted himself into the sanctuary.

"Come in, Mike!" Brown said. "I've asked Mike to join us."

"Why?" McBride said.

"He knows more about this kind of business than I do."

"Nice to see you too," Joyce said to McBride, and seated himself stiffly in the last empty blue throne, like Lincoln in his monument — if Lincoln looked like a balding retired hockey legend.

Marks came from the bar with a tray of drinks and passed them around.

"Champagne cocktails!" Brown said. "Whets the appetite. Cold and refreshing. You've had a hard day, I expect. Cheers, everyone!"

"We didn't learn much," McBride said. "Your brother is—"

Brown silenced him with his traffic-stopping mudra. "Just a moment. How long till dinner, George?"

He didn't want Marks to know about the case.

"Jackie says dinner will be served shortly."

Everyone was on a first-name basis.

Marks excused himself.

"Now, you were saying?" Brown said.

"Even George doesn't know about this business?"

"This is personal. Did you make any progress today? What did you do?"

"George doesn't know any of your personal business?"

Brown gave Joyce a very quick glance. "Not this personal."

"Aside from the four of us, and Lobb, who is read in?"

"Read in?"

"Cora doesn't know why you're working for *us* now," Joyce said.

"Then she knows that I am on the payroll?" McBride replied to Brown, not Joyce.

Brown checked in with Joyce again, not quite as briefly this time.

"Is she tailing me again?" McBride said.

"No," Joyce said.

"Is anyone else?"

"Nobody who works for us."

"Why are *you* here then?"

Joyce's face marbled.

"I already told you that," Brown said, then smiled. "Let's be easy. You're part of the team now."

"Oh gee, coach, thanks. You're swell."

Joyce leaned forward and looked at him hard. "I can't make out whether pissing people off is the only way you know how to get information out of them or if you just can't help being an asshole by nature."

"Mike!" Brown said, a gentle edge in his voice now. "McBride. Let's focus on the case, shall we?"

Joyce obediently eased back a few degrees, like a trigger being unsqueezed.

"So what did you do today?" Brown said. "What did you learn?"

McBride hesitated, drained his cocktail.

Sylvia crossed her legs the other way.

"Well," McBride said, "we visited the subject's last known address, and we—"

"Where is that?" Joyce said.

"*And,*" (speaking to Brown) "we interviewed all known associates."

"Who are they?" Joyce said.

"*And,*" (still speaking to Brown) "basically, we learned nothing important."

"Nothing?" Brown said.

"Well, it's only the first day."

"That's it?" Joyce said.

"Yes," Sylvia said. "So far. That's it."

"I want to see written reports."

"What's your plan for tomorrow?" Brown said.

"More of the same," McBride said calmly. "One thing leads to another."

"I want to see the names, addresses, dates, and notes of interviews," Joyce said. "Just like a real investigator."

"Something I've been wondering about, Mike: who dresses you? I've seldom seen a man look less remarkable. Are you trying to impress Miss Cora? Does she go for the ultra-drab look? I guess I read her all wrong."

Joyce leaned forward again, bringing the full force of his ordinary face to bear on McBride's quizzical smirk. "Shut your mouth. Do your job. File your report. Collect your check. Get out." He swung the beam of his scowl across to Sylvia. "Same for you, Little Miss High-and-Tight. You think the two of you can handle that?"

"Well, that seems clear enough," McBride said, completely clarified. "What do you say, High-and-Tight, shall we get back to finding the fellow that Mr. and Mrs. Drab couldn't manage with a map?"

Sylvia said nothing but she looked like she was struggling not to hock up a turnip.

Brown lifted both evil-averting palms. "I want all three of you to calm down and remember who the boss is here. Your alpha-male battle is childish and boring. Let's get back to work. All right? All right. But first, I see it's time to eat."

Marks had just returned, and now announced dinner.

"And while we're at it," Brown said, "let's drink and be merry, goddamn it."

He led them out and back to the public part of the house, into a vaulted dining hall off the main ballroom. They picked up Angus en route, waiting outside the last locked door to the private wing. In the dining hall a long banquet table was laid in white china on white cloth. About a dozen people were sitting around it tucking in, while as many others swarmed around them forking food from the platters and bowls onto their plates, which they carried off to the ballroom, or they milled about the table and ate standing, or sat down against the wall on the royal blue carpet. There were magnums of champagne in silver ice-buckets on sideboards. The digestive harmonies of smooth jazz piped in from speakers hidden in the walls. The scene reminded McBride of the loose loud ambiance of the second half of the financial district Christmas parties his wife used to drag him to.

They had lost Joyce en route. When she noticed it Sylvia said, aside to McBride, "I do hope it was something you said."

Brown had the only assigned seat, in the middle of the table, rather than the head. But the setting was waiting for him and so it seemed was the party, idling until he arrived and took up his post, then shifted into drive and started down the night. Angus crossed to a spot in the corner reserved for him, perched himself on a stool, and balanced a plate of vegetables on a crossed knee.

McBride and Sylvia carried off two mountains of food and looked for a place to talk apart.

CHAPTER 53

DEVELOPMENT

They split up later. A local cover band called *In Full* had been hired for the evening to infuse the ballroom with classic rock nostalgia. Sylvia accepted an invitation from a pair of blondes in miniskirts to dance. McBride wandered into the game room to watch the Red Sox season opener on an enormous monitor. Pale beer and roasted peanuts were available in bucketfuls. Everyone was laughing and shouting mindlessly. At the other end of the room men in oxford shirts and Bermuda shorts were betting fives and tens on games of eight ball; the crack of the breaks and pockets punctuated the game commentary with a satisfyingly solid noise.

In the bottom of the fourth inning the score was still *nada de nada* when Cora Lobb entered the room. McBride was feeling too relaxed and good-humored to abandon his comfortable chair. He even let her see him watching her — the way, he hoped, a hanging judge might watch a perp on the stand. Nevertheless, after hesitating a moment, she came over, beer in hand, turned a loose chair around and straddled it facing him. She leaned in close and spoke quietly.

"I went into the pub that night," she said, "so I could see who you were meeting. The only thing I was told about the job was that you were looking for Mr. Brown and Mr. Brown wanted to know why, who you were working for. I wasn't planning to fuck you. I wasn't even planning to talk to you. But you didn't meet anyone and you didn't seem to be waiting for anyone, and you noticed me, so I just, well I just thought I'd let you hit on me and see if I could get anything. Which was stupid. I should have known better. I knew you were a pro. Maybe I just wanted to talk to you anyway. And then I let it get it out of hand. Because I liked you. I thought you were clever. I liked the way you looked at me and the way you talked to me. And it was stupid. And unprofessional."

"Depends on your profession, doesn't it?"

"I deserve that. I feel like that too. I've felt like an absolute shit ever since. I'm sorry."

"Swell."

"I just don't want you to think that's what I do."

"What do you care what I think?"

"Most of the time I'm just a mild-mannered research assistant. I take calls, I keep accounts, I do legwork, I run background checks."

"For Joyce or Brown?"

"I work for Mike. Mike works for Mr. Brown."

"Ever sleep with him?"

"No."

"Which one?"

"Neither one."

"Does Brownie have a regular squeeze? Or is it strictly on rotation?"

Cora looked down at her feet.

McBride pressed, brutally. "Well?"

"What do you care?"

"He hired me to work his side of the case now. So that's what I'm doing. Don't you want to be helpful?"

Her small sky-blue eyes welled up now, but didn't spill over, and her face stayed hard.

"I want to ask you something," she said. "When did you figure it out?"

"What, that you were a whore?"

She winced. She didn't try not to. She wasn't tough, and she didn't pretend to be tough.

"I knew the score before you said hello," McBride said.

"That's a lie." No, she wasn't tough, but she wasn't timid either.

"Yes," he admitted. Point, Cora. "I started figuring it out the next morning."

"How?"

"Are you asking me to critique your performance?"

"Sometimes, Mick, you can just answer a question. It's not like admitting defeat to just answer a damn question."

That stung. Not because she was right, though she was, but because it reminded him why he had liked her. The bullshit and the beauty get mixed up together. You try to pretend it's all bullshit, but that's not the part you fell for when you fell, and you can't forget that without going dead. These are your choices — death or suffering.

"You made too many small mistakes. You're not a natural liar and you didn't have time to prepare your role. Most people can't wing it like that, not that deep, not without training and preparation."

"Be specific. I want to know."

"First, I'm not that hot. I try not to be. Nobody looks like you goes that hard for a guy like me. And nobody leaves their car behind. Nobody is that impulsive that isn't half a flake, or more, and you're not half a flake or more. It's hard to hide intelligence, especially when you know it's your hook, and intelligent women don't ask strange men to take them in. And it was a lot of little things too — well, a *few* little things that added up to too much:

your overnight bag was too clean and too light, the shirt you changed into was brand new and it wasn't your style."

"When did you know for sure?"

"On the drive up. You tried too hard to keep me interested so I wouldn't start to think about what was going on. The best way to get a good detective's attention is to distract him."

She listened carefully, like she cared, like she was disappointed she hadn't impressed him better, like there could ever be another chance.

"You are good, you know," she said. "You know how I knew you'd made me? Because you can't fake what you are. You couldn't pull off the asshole hit-it-and-quit-it act. You don't have it in you to be that small. You knew the score and played the right notes, but you didn't feel the music. I don't know who you're really working for or what you're really looking for, and I don't care. But, I—" She seemed to lose her thought for a moment. "But I—" Picked it up again — "If I could do it over, I wouldn't have—" Her voice caught.

"Wouldn't have done it over?"

"If I had been in that bar for any other reason — I wish I could have been — I wish we could have been—"

"Life is tricky like that, Cora. You mostly don't get do-overs. You just get fucked. I think I read that on a fortune cookie."

"Bastard." Two tears escaped her eyes. She didn't look away or hide them. She didn't play them either. McBride watched the two bright drops slip through the freckles of her broad flat cheeks and trip over the sharp line of her upper lip into her mouth. He saw that she wanted to punish him for hurting her. But that was the end of it. His mouth tightened. There could be no undoing now. Just for an instant a softness flashed in his eyes before he looked away from her and pretended to watch the Sox strike out of the fifth inning and go to commercial.

CHAPTER 54

THE MARRYING MAIDEN

After the game — Red Sox 1, White Sox 2 — McBride went to bed. He'd lost track of Sylvia and hoped that she had already turned in, but the room was empty. He hesitated. He didn't know if he needed permission to get into that bed without her. The whole situation was completely jacked up. Last night they had necked on the couch like teenagers then shared a bed like strangers. Today she didn't want to talk about it. The vision of her in the shower this morning had been stuck in his head all day. Maybe it was all right to go to bed. Maybe she wasn't going to sleep in this room tonight anyway. Maybe she went home. She'd been avoiding him all evening.

He sat down in a reading chair in the darkness in the white room and took off his boots. He checked his phone for messages from her. Nothing. He typed out several to send her—

— are you coming to bed, syl?

— what's the plan?

— I'm turning in. You?

— nightcap?

— where the hell are you?

But sent nothing.

His mind drifted. He tried to think about the case, the Brothers Bizarre, but it wouldn't hold his attention. He wanted to know what she was doing. He started to put his boots back on and go down to find her, changed his mind before he had them tied, kicked them off again, and threw them across the room.

They came up against a bookcase, and he went to it hopefully, using the light on his phone to scan the spines — a jumble of topics:

Blue and Gray: A Short History of the War Between the States.
Time and Space: A Love Story.
The Martian Women.
The Faerie Queene.
Romanticism: Poetry and Criticism.
The Brothers Karamazov.
Economics for Idiots.
Oahspe: A New Bible.
Calculus for Engineers.
Nietzsche: Essential Writings.

He took that one back to his seat and turned on the reading lamp. Zarathustra was always good for a distraction.

"Everything straight lies," murmured the Dwarf disdainfully. *"All Truth is crooked, Time itself is a circle."*

"Amen, brother," he whispered.

"From this gateway Moment a long eternal lane runs back: an Eternity lies behind us. Must not all things that can run have already run along this Lane? Must not all things that can happen have already happened, been done, run past?"

He made up his mind that Sylvia should find him sitting there reading, wide awake, fully clothed, not in the bed.

"And if all things have been here before: what do you think of this Moment, Dwarf? Must not this Gateway, too, have been here — before? And are not all things bound fast together in such a way that this Moment draws after it all future things?"

· · ·

McBride woke with a start, gasping, his neck stiff, the lamp glaring down on his face like an interrogation. Sylvia was in bed asleep. His head was pounding. He looked at his phone. He'd been out a couple of hours. Why didn't she wake him up? He looked at her again. Was she really asleep?

"You asleep?" he said quietly.

Not even a twitch. Fuck it. Go to bed. He turned off the lamp, stripped to his briefs, took a piss, climbed up the bed, and tucked himself him in without touching her.

CHAPTER 55

ABUNDANCE

The screaming gates of heaven woke him far too early. McBride groaned and rolled dead onto his back and threw his arm across his eyes. He heard Sylvia move.

"You awake?" he said softly.

"Yeah."

He peaked from under his elbow. She had her hands behind her head staring into the blinding white air. Her shoulders above the snow white coverlet were bare. He rolled toward her and lifted the blanket for a peek.

"Knock it off," she said matter-of-factly, without turning her head.

He dropped the blanket like a snake and propped his head on his hand. The sunlight thundered into his brain.

"What are you thinking about?"

"All sorts of things." She still didn't look at him. "Wondering what Gray is up to. I don't think he just ran. Not when he's this close. He's got to be looking for another way in."

"Yeah well whatever. What about us?"

"Us? Oh, I don't know. I can't think about that right now."

"What's going on with you? Night before last you were all over me."

"I was drunk."

"Come on, don't play games."

"Look, I don't know. It just happened."

"Yeah it just happened. Why did it just happen then when it never just happened before?"

"I don't know. I was horny. You were there."

"Any cock would do?"

She still didn't look at him. "Fuck you."

"Fuck you back."

Now she did. "I don't know. I don't know why I climbed into the sack with Morris either. This damn case. It's messing with both our heads."

"You mean we both got laid and we both feel jealous."

"I mean we both got burned and we both feel vulnerable."

"Or maybe we both got reminded who we can depend on."

"Can we just let it lie for now? Just work the case for now. Go back to being the mild-mannered research assistant and the tough old shamus?"

"I'm not that old."

"You're not that tough."

"Fuck you."

"Fuck you back."

He threw off the sweltering clouds. "I'm getting in the shower then."

When he returned she was gone.

He called her cell but she didn't answer.

He dressed and called again. No answer.

A knock at the door.

McBride grabbed the handle and threw the door open. "How did you know I was up?"

Marks smiled his forbearing smile. "Good morning, Mr. McBride. Will you be joining Mr. Brown again at breakfast?"

CHAPTER 56

THE WANDERER

Admitted into the Presence. McBride stalked in and sat down roughly.

The Great Man collapsed his newspaper and spoke: "Good morning, old boy!" — irradiating another white morning with his blazing smile. Fire on Phosphorous Mountain.

In the pond below, the swan pair upended like fangs. A steady wind brushed through the dark cedars that shielded the pool.

Two places were laid, not three.

Brown lay his paper aside on the spot where Sylvia yesterday had eaten her bagel. "Where's your partner in crime this morning?"

Marks filled McBride's cup from the coffeepot on the table. "What would you like for breakfast?"

"This will do," McBride said, meaning what was standing on the table. "Go away, George."

Marks dropped the pot, glanced for permission at Brown, and vacated.

"First," McBride said, "nobody says 'old boy.' It's not even quaint. At best it's silly, at worst pretentious. Second, your people gave Sylvia a ride somewhere so you know better than me where she is. Third, ask me another stupid question and I'm off the case and you're on your own. So how about we cut the shit and get to work?"

There was a twinkle in Brown's eye. McBride couldn't make out whether it was mischief or merriment. "Sleep well?"

McBride snapped at his coffee, spilling it on his chin. It was hot and he let it burn. Sitting here was masochism. Participating in this absurd fraternal hide-and-seek was masochism. Coffee was nothing.

"You're in a dark mood," Brown said. "But let's go to a Bruins game tonight. How about it?"

"Swell. Maybe we'll get our picture in the paper."

The twinkle vanished. "That's not funny, McBride. Now what do you have planned for today?"

"Keep on keeping on. I know a psychic I could consult."

"A psychic?" Brown disapproved.

"You're the one said detectives are diviners. If that doesn't work out I might try a priest."

"Seriously, McBride."

"Seriously, follow the money. It's the hardest kind of thing to hide."

"You're a cynic. Do you think *every*thing is for sale?"

"No. But the things that don't matter generally are. And those are the things that people hire me to hunt."

CHAPTER 57

THE GENTLE WIND

Having nothing better to do with the day, McBride spent it at the Strip by Strega, Boston's next dining experience, an ultra-modern Italian steakhouse, in the Park Plaza, at a corner window table where he could keep an eye on the main entrance to Gray's bank across the street, two blocks down from the Taj. His idea was that changing banks was harder than changing hotels and when Gray needed money he'd have to pay a visit on his safe-deposit box. It was a long shot but it was something to do while he called every other hotel in town looking for him. He called the most expensive joints first, giving them all one pretext or another—

"Morning. Humphrey Bogart, FedEx. Got a priority package for, uh, Mr. Morrie Green, Gray, something like that, care of Ritz Carlton? Label is smudged. That you fellas?"

Between cold-calling hotels, he phoned or texted Sylvia. She never answered or responded. He left her a voicemail saying Brown had invited them to the Bruins game tonight and he hoped she'd come.

Gray never turned up. It was a long dry windy day. McBride kept up his strength alternating between coffee and beer until the bank closed. His server was a sturdy Chinese woman who called herself Joy Dui and looked like everybody's eldest sister. 5' 5", 150 lbs., 50. When she discovered McBride spoke Mandarin she became friendly.

For dinner he ordered one of the chief culinarian's newest dining experiences, ate it contemplatively, gave Joy Dui a hug on his way out, flagged down a taxi and went home.

CHAPTER 58

THE JOYOUS LAKE

As soon as he got back to Peabody, McBride pulled his shell across the smiling lake to Sylvia's property. She wasn't home and her car was gone. He called her again, and again got no answer. He went back down to the water and ripped a couple of furious laps before it got too dark, then headed for home and got in the shower.

He was trying her again when he saw through the window Brown's black Suburban pull into the cul-de-sac. The beefy bodyguard, in a gray suit, rolled out of the front passenger door, scanned the area for threats, and stalked up the drive around the Office. McBride timed yanking the door open so that his knock landed on air.

"Hello, Holstein!" he said with prodigious good fellowship.

The Angus swept his lifted knuckles aside like he was parrying a punch to the face. "Mr. Brown would like to come in, if that's all right with you."

"Swell! Send him in!"

Angus looked flatly at McBride for several seconds, waiting for him to get the picture.

McBride mulled a moment and decided to acquiesce. Maybe he'd learn something. He stepped aside silently and extended his arm in welcome and the bodyguard shouldered past him and made a quick inspection. Foyer, check. Living room/kitchen, check. Back porch, check. He went up the stairs two at a time. The ceiling creaked cheerfully under his step. McBride left the front door standing open and crossed through to the other end of the foyer and leaned against the corner at the foot of the stairs.

"While you're up there, sport," he called, "would you mind being a help and cleaning the toilet?"

No answer.

"If everyone pitches in and does their part, we can make the crapper a better experience for everybody."

Angus came back to the head of the stairs and spoke down to him: "Do you keep weapons in the house?"

"Sure."

"Where?"

"Kitchen drawer. Butcher knife, couple of steak knives, a heavy pewter mug with a good stout handle on it."

Angus started down the stairs slowly, like an enormous Slinky.

"Oh, also, in the basement there's a hammer, a pry bar, a box cutter, some pliers. You can fuck a brother up with a good pair of pliers."

Angus stopped on the last step, apparently trying to loom over him. "Where's your gun?"

McBride gave him a come-hither wink. "I'll show you mine if you show me yours." He eyed the bulge under Angus's left arm, then the bulge between his legs. He saw both the hard hands curl halfway into fists.

"Relax, honey," McBride said, looking away again, unconcerned, still leaning against the wall. "I don't do virgins. — Now go tell your master you cased the joint and he's welcome to visit now or anytime."

The bodyguard took the last step down and swung the slab of his body around the stairpost and lumbered lightly back outside.

The opaque rear window came down and there was a brief chat between him and the occupants of the back seat. Angus shrugged and nodded and opened the door and Brown popped out of it like a slice of cheese between two well-toasted women. Leaving the car door open, Angus led them, laughing (them, not him), up the drive back to the house. Brown and the women sported black and gold Bruins jerseys and champagne flutes. Let the sacred rites begin.

McBride watched it all through the front door, which was still standing open.

The bodyguard stepped aside at the threshold and let his wards enter the house before him.

Brown smiled big and opened his arms and threatened to embrace him, drink in hand. "We thought we'd like to see the joint!"

It was the battle of the bonhomie. McBride retreated. "The *joint*?" Angus must have relayed his message verbatim.

"The headquarters of the organization! The hub. The station. The precinct house. The place where the magic happens."

Bodyguard came in last and shut the door and made like a tree planted by the waters. He shall not be moved.

"Anyway, hello, old boy!" Brown beamed. "Are you ready to worship at the house of the holy hockey puck?"

"Sure."

Brown plucked from the oak's right limb an extra jersey (number 17, Lucic, left wing), and handed it to McBride. "This is for you." From the left he took the bottle they were drinking and an empty glass and handed the glass to McBride and emptied the bottle into it and hung the bottle back on the tree. "Cheers!"

They all clinked.

"Let me introduce you to our escorts this evening," Brown said. "This is Annie and this is Alice. Alice and Annie, Christian McBride, who doesn't care for his *Christian* name. Get it? You can call him McBride. Or Chris. Or *Christ*, if he's *really* hitting your spot."

Alice and Annie were the women from the hockey photo. Twins, no less. Pretty and perky and probably under thirty. A pair of cliches in high heels and hockey shirts.

"We saw you around the house last night," Alice said, and gave him a hug.

"We met your friend Sylvia!" Annie said and also gave him a hug.

"I heard."

"She is an excellent dancer," Alice said.

"And so mysterious and sultry," Annie said.

"She's a peach," McBride said. Leaving the mighty oak standing in the foyer, he ushered them into the living room/kitchen.

Brown declared, "It's charming, McBride! It's you all over." He crossed through to the bookcases that filled the opposite wall.

"Oh, isn't this the cutest refrigerator?" Alice said, stroking the round red shoulders of the old box. "So retro!"

"That it is," McBride said. "If you reach inside you're liable to find leftovers from 1972."

"You're right," she said to Brown, "he's funny."

"Why," Brown said over his shoulder, "what's funny about 1972?"

"Nixon was funny," McBride said.

"You were twelve. And in China."

"Nixon was big in China. He made even Mao look respectable."

"Mao was a psychopath."

"So was Nixon."

"Watergate."

"Vietnam."

"Munich Olympics."

"Where was John Brown in '72?"

Brown glanced back. "Don't you read anything for fun?" he said. "Or maybe you think *The World as Will and Representation* is fun. Oh, and here's a ripping yarn, *A Daoist History of Chinese Thought*."

"I don't come to your house and criticize your art collection."

"How could you? I have excellent taste. Don't you like my Greek marbles?"

"Are those the naked white ones?" McBride said. Brown was an ass, but he was comical. Speaking of ass, he thought, admiring the twins.

"The Maltese Falcon!" said Annie, admiring the replica black raptor perched atop the fridge.

"That dingus was my going away present when I retired from the force."

"It's cute!"

(It still had the evidence room tag the boys and girls had tied around its legs — scrawled on the back: *Found this on a body. Thought you might like it. — The Crew.*)

Brown and the twins laughingly inspected "the joint" for a while, declaring every dead cockroach and dust ball just darling and charming, until Brown decided it was time to roll out to the big game. The Bruins were in the playoffs. Game one.

CHAPTER 59

DISPERSION

Brown had season tickets for a row of five front-row-corner seats at the Garden. The photographers' well was in the opposite corner, the spot from which Gray's photo had been snapped. There was some silly byplay between Brown and his guard over who would sit where. The guard had to be on the aisle, Brown wanted McBride between the women, the guard didn't want Brown at the opposite end of the row. They worked it out, from aisle to center: Angus, Brown, Alice, McBride, and Annie against the rail.

The Canadiens took the initiative out of the box, keeping Rask dancing and darting for shot after shot.

McBride took a picture with his phone and messaged it to Sylvia. *Here with JB and friends. Wish you were.*

Brown and the escort twins were really into the game, jumping up every time Montreal got close to the net, shouting, grabbing each other. Annie would throw her arm over McBride's shoulder for extra leverage jumping up and down. McBride was her rock, her fulcrum. Every time the Bruins successfully defended another attack and cleared the ice she yelled "Yeah!" and grabbed him.

Every time a Canadien skated near their corner the twins hammered open hands on the glass.

The Bruins never managed to pull together much of an offense in the first period and somehow got out of it without giving up a goal. Rask skated for the locker room like a man limping away from a burning car.

Annie and McBride headed for the restrooms, promising to return with cool beer and warm pretzels. Annie hooked her fingers into the waistband of his jeans so he could help haul her up the concrete stairs. 5000 other people were also filtering out through the gates, so their progress was erratic. She seemed to like to run into him from behind. Coming up to the platform she gave his ass a squeeze.

"Nice butt!" she said, close to his ear.

"Thanks. I got it cheap on eBay."

"You never say anything straight!"

"It's a tic."

They separated in the corridor to find their respective restrooms, arranging to meet at the same spot.

First game of the playoffs, packed house, major rivalry, everybody shouting: you couldn't walk without tripping over other feet. McBride figured the playoffs would be finished before they got back to their seats.

The restroom smelled like sour beer and piss. There was a queue for the urinals. Most of the men didn't bother to wash their hands. McBride made a ritual gesture. Somebody in a hurry kicked his heel and he stumbled and caught himself on a sink.

Somebody yelled, "Tripping! Two minutes!" Laughter.

In the mirror over the sinks McBride caught a glance of the offender looking back at him as he ducked out — some pudgy middle-ager in a game jersey, his hairless head and face completely covered in black and gold greasepaint, half and half like a theatre mask, red eyes glancing out from under paint-heavy lids. Four seconds later, as McBride was wetting his hands, it hit him who was hiding under that face paint. Morris Fucking Gray.

He jumped outside, hands wet, and tried to guess which way Gray had gone — but it was too late, and the crowd was too thick. McBride ducked right at random and cut through the crowd as fast as he could manage without starting a fight, but he caught no glimpse of Gray. He slowed down and worked his way methodically all the way around the circular corridor, asking every security cop along the way if they'd seen a bald male, six foot, 45, 200 pounds, Bruins jersey, black and gold face paint, in a hurry. Nothing. Gray had vanished. Probably taken the stairs and left the building.

By the time he got back to his starting point he'd missed his rendezvous with Annie and the second period had started. He went back in and headed down to their seats, but encountered Brown and company ascending in haste, Angus the Angry in the lead, barking into a cell phone.

"We're leaving," Brown said as he brushed past McBride. He looked scared.

McBride fell in ahead of Annie.

"Where'd you go?" she said.

In the corridor, Brown seemed to be restraining himself from breaking into a run.

McBride trotted to catch up to him.

"What's going on?" he said. "Did you see him?"

"The photo — See who?" Brown said.

"The prodigal brother. I just tripped over him in the john."

Brown shied away from this news like a running deer bouncing off a pickup truck, stumbled, caught himself, looked wildly around for the enemy, and shoved Angus in the shoulder. "Hurry the fuck up."

They were walking so fast they were attracting the attention of the security cops, who were probably also recognizing McBride from interrogating them a few minutes earlier. But the party was back to the exits in half a minute and found the Suburban, signaled by Angus's call, rushing up the street and stopping hard in front of them without pulling over. Angus flung open a door and bulldogged Brown in through it. McBride, Annie, and Alice barely had time to get inside themselves before the driver took off, letting momentum slam the doors to. McBride could tell the getaway procedure had been practiced to perfection.

Catching his breath, McBride said, "What gives?"

"What happened?" Brown said, his voice breaking loud. "Did you fucking set me up?"

"Set you up for what?"

"Did you tell him we were going to be here tonight?"

"Don't be stupid. Did you see him?"

Alice and Annie cowered at one end of the couch seats. Angus sat close to Brown, leaning forward, focused on McBride, ready to strike if necessary. McBride made his face hard and sat back in his seat, ready to duck if necessary.

"How did he know I was here?" Brown said, still nearly shouting.

"I don't know that he did," McBride said, his voice cold. "He told me before that he's been trolling home games for you."

Brown threw his hands up wildly. "Why the fuck didn't you tell me that before?"

"I passed him in the restroom. He was in face paint. It didn't hit me for a second who it was. By then he'd vanished."

"Are you sure it was him?" He looked ghastly. Pale with fear.

"Yeah. The fact that he ran or hid confirms it. He couldn't have disappeared that fast unless he meant to. When's the last game you went to?"

"I don't know! A month ago. Maybe more."

"He could have nailed you any time. It's pretty easy to tell from the photo where your seats are. My guess is he's always known who you are, and he's been tailing you for weeks, maybe months. My theory is he took the photo himself and hired me just to spook you."

"The photo! Fuck. Fuck. Fuck. Fuck." He repeated this mantra over and over again for half a minute.

"The photo! The photo!" McBride mocked. "What the hell is going on, John?"

"The photo, you idiot! The fucking photo." Another long burst of fucks ensued, like he was thumbing a rosary.

"For Christ's sake, what about it?"

"It just happened! The play in your fucking photo. It just happened, right in front of us." Brown was on the verge of tears, his voice almost a wail.

McBride finally clued in: the scene in Gray's hockey photo — the defender airborne over the Bruin, their four legs making an X — had just happened. "Oh, come on, John. That's impossible." It gave him a sudden chill. That feeling you get whenever you remember nobody ever gets out of this world alive and neither will you.

"How the fuck do you know what's possible!" Brown yelled. "Stop the car! Stop the car!"

The driver slammed to a stop in the middle of Storrow Drive.

"Get the fuck out, McBride. — Give him a bill."

Angus produced another hundred from the endless roll in his pocket and stabbed it at McBride.

"Get a cab home," Brown said. "Or whatever. Just get the fuck out. You're fired."

McBride took the bill mechanically.

Angus shoved the door open and dared McBride with a look to hesitate so he could toss him through it.

The traffic balled up behind them started honking.

McBride slid out. He felt dizzy. "Good night, John," he said, standing in the street. "It's been surreal—"

The Suburban sprang away into the night.

McBride was still wearing number 17.

Somebody threw a water bottle at him from the next car, but it missed.

CHAPTER 60

LIMITATION

Dawn came shrouded in cold rain. McBride had slept fitfully, and not at all since 0400. At 0530 — he was watching the clock — it was just growing light and he gave it up altogether. He'd slept with his piece on the bedside table and now as he rose from his brooding he picked it up and carried it downstairs to make coffee. In the midst of that fumbling task somebody knocked on the door. He put his right hand on the gun lying on the countertop and yelled, "I'm in the kitchen!"

He heard the door open and the threshold creak.

"Who is it!"

"It's me!" Sylvia.

She squeaked through the foyer on wet shoes and into the room. She was soaked through, her hair black and slick, her nipples popped through her shirt, her skin pale and blotched. She noticed the gun on the counter beside the sink where he was rinsing out the coffeepot.

"Expecting trouble?"

"I ought to shoot you now," he said.

"Making coffee? I'm frozen."

"You told Gray we were at the game last night."

"Yeah, I told him," she said as she kicked her squishy running shoes off. "Now I'm going upstairs to get a towel and dry off. Then you can shoot me."

"I plan to. You want coffee first?"

He put the pot on to drip and went outside to sit on the porch. The rain was falling grey and steady, a shimmering curtain obscuring the pond below the yard.

Sylvia joined him a few minutes later, carrying two brown mugs. She had changed into a pair of McBride's sweatpants and a torn red flannel shirt. They were far too big for her, of course. She sat down in the other Adirondack chair and folded her legs up in front of her, bare toes dangling off the front of the chair.

"I should leave a change of clothes over here," she said.

"You're not going to need them after I shoot you."

"These are your own clothes, McBee. You'll get them all bloody. — What's up with that anyway?" The Walther was now resting unholstered on the wood slats of the table between their chairs.

"Something weird happened. Where's my boat?" The trestles before the porch stood empty.

"I borrowed it," she said. "It's at my place. I was going to bring it back this morning, but I didn't want to go out on the lake in the rain, so I jogged around instead."

"To tell me what?"

"That I'm sorry for how I acted yesterday."

"You should be. But there's something else."

"And that Joyce was tailing me all day yesterday."

"That explains why I didn't see him. And I'm hearing a third headline coming too."

"So that's why I needed the boat. I wanted him to think I was here. I snuck out the back and rowed across to my place."

"OK, what's the third thing?"

"Gray wants us to arrange another meet."

"Fuck Gray."

"He'll give you the hundred grand."

"Fuck Gray."

"In advance."

"Where is he?"

"My place. That's why I wanted Joyce to think I was here."

"Your place? Well, that's fucking perfect. How long has he been there?"

"He showed up last night around two."

"These guys sure pick swell hours to do their visiting. What is it with them and two a.m.? You were expecting him, weren't you?"

"Yes. He's in bad shape."

"I bet. What's the setup?"

"Morris wants to meet Brown here — at your place."

"You have the money yet?"

"I saw it. He has it in a gym bag. It's on the living room floor."

"Brown will never go for it."

"Come on, McBee. You can charm him into it."

"He fired me."

"Oh."

"God damn it, Sylvia. Were you at the game too? Did you fuck him again? Have you been in touch with him all along? I'm really pissed off at you."

"I'm sorry. I panicked."

"So it's over with us?"

She hesitated before answering. "I hope not. I don't want it to be."

McBride started several times to respond, but bit off each reply unspoken.

Finally Sylvia said, "Well, what happened at the game?"

He gave her the play-by-play. He noticed as he talked that he gave more than due importance to the way the twins had flirted with him. It was childish, but he indulged himself. It had no apparent effect.

"Oh yeah," she said, "I ran into them the night before at Brown's everlasting party."

"Why didn't you tell me?"

"I didn't think that much of it. The women he goes to games with. I figured you'd seen them too. We were all the same place."

"You should have told me."

"What difference would it make?"

"Did you even question them?"

"No. I was dancing and getting high."

"You were working."

"You were sulking in the room reading fucking Nietzsche."

"Fuck—"

"You back." She sipped her coffee meditatively while McBride fumed. "Well, so what happened next? How did the evening end?"

"Then I used the bill that Beefstick threw at me to flag down a cab and came home and went to bed."

"So you didn't actually see the play," she said.

"No, but I saw the look in Brown's eyes after."

"It doesn't make any sense."

"Nothing about this fucking case has made any sense from the word go."

"It's got to be a setup."

"For what?"

"It's a gag. Somebody is punking you big time."

"Who? If it's you, I *will* shoot you. Come to think of it, the first time Morris called me I thought it was a gag. Two in the fucking morning. You put one of your silly-ass actor friends up to it."

She gave him a concerned look. "Don't make me say it."

McBride paused for coffee. "I'm still going to shoot you. As soon as I finish this cup. I won't kill you, because that's too much fucking red tape. But I'll put one through your foot. It'll hurt. A lot. And it'll keep you from kicking my ass."

"Don't count on it."

"You might be right about it being a gag though. What if Morris paid a player to take a dive in Brown's corner? It wouldn't have to be perfect, just similar enough to spook the hell out of him."

"Seems pretty far-fetched. And why?"

"Because the play's the thing to catch the conscience of the kin. And because he's nuts."

"More likely Brown is having you on. You didn't see it. He's got you going."

"Why?"

"Maybe he thought he could scare you into something. I don't know."

"It was a pretty convincing act. You should have seen the way they hustled his ass out of there. It was like extracting the president. They had a routine. Who practices escape maneuvers with their bodyguards?"

"Executive politicians."

"And rich paranoids."

"So let's get it over with. Why don't you go ahead and call J.B. Get him over here somehow. Take the money and run."

"I've got to get this fucking case out of my head." He picked up his phone. It was a few minutes past 6:00 a.m. He hoped Brown was asleep.

CHAPTER 61

INNER TRUTH

The black Suburban arrived an hour later with Joyce's white Ford pickup in tow.

Joyce and Cora exited either side of the pickup, the Angry Holstein from the right front door of the Suburban. Standing in a tight circle in the blowing silver rain, the three of them ostentatiously surveyed the surrounding cul-de-sac before swimming ponderously up the grey gravel drive to the house.

McBride stood in the open door and watched their playacting.

"Are you armed?" Angus said.

"Yes."

"Why don't you put your gun down on the floor."

"Why don't you kiss my sweet ass."

"Why don't I break your nose."

"Because I'll shoot you."

Angus mulled his options for two long seconds. "Step back. We need to check the place."

"For what?"

From behind Angus, Joyce said, "Let's get this over with."

From behind Joyce, Cora avoided eye contact.

McBride stepped back and they trooped in. "Wipe your feet."

They found Sylvia in the living room, sitting sideways at the little drop-leaf table against the back window.

Joyce said, "Have you been here all night?"

"Of course," she said. "Fucked our brains out. Did you get any good pics?"

Joyce's persistent frown deepened slightly. "What is it with you two? Act like professionals."

Sylvia gave him a chilling look.

Joyce looked away at McBride. "Where's your man?"

"He's not our man," McBride said, sitting down on the other side of the table from Sylvia.

"He's not here yet," Sylvia said.

Joyce let a heavy breath escape him, waiting for the rest.

"You can frisk him before he comes inside," McBride said.

Joyce and company sniffed the house from top to bottom, back to front — all three rooms, basement, and porch.

McBride and Sylvia waited in the living room.

McBride said, "Think 'our man' will show this time?"

"He'll show."

Joyce and Cora left Angus in the foyer and walked out to the Suburban to report their findings.

Joyce returned after a minute and told McBride that Brown wanted to talk to him. McBride followed him back down the drive again to the Suburban. McBride stood in the rain, talking to Brown over the half-lowered tinted glass. Joyce stood at his elbow. Cora had gotten in the back with Brown.

Brown said, "You've been playing me all along, haven't you, McBride? You've been in touch with him all along. You set this whole thing up."

"I guess you finally figured it out, John. And I might as well tell you I took the photo last night too."

Brown ignored his sarcasm. "Well where is he?"

"He'll be along."

"When?"

"When I call him."

"So call him."

"When we're all inside."

"Why?"

"Because I said so."

"Mike says you're armed."

"So's Mike. And the beefsteak. And probably the chauffeur. And yourself." He looked deeper inside the cabin. "What about you, Cora, you packin' heat too?"

She looked at him, sullenly, and did not reply.

"Mike says he doesn't like the setup," Brown said.

Joyce confirmed: "I don't like it."

"You want some assurance of my sincerity?" McBride said. "Well, I'm wet and cold and bored. You can come in and bring all your muscle with you, or you can go away and wait for your secret brother to decide to try again. I get paid the same either way."

"He paid you to set this up?"

"No, John, I just really like twins. It's the symmetry."

He turned away and walked back up to the house, brushed by Angus at the front door, went to the kitchen and poured himself another cup of coffee, and rejoined Sylvia at the drop-leaf table.

They could see through the far window Joyce standing beside the Suburban, still talking to Brown. His body language, such as it was, communicated stubborn disagreement. Perhaps that was the push that tilted the scale the other way: Brown liked to be the boss.

Joyce submitted, shrugged slightly, opened the door for Brown and stepped back. Brown got out cautiously, stopped, turned back. Apparently Cora wanted to wait in the car. Brown said no, but she didn't get out. Joyce shut the door, and Brown came up the drive behind him, nervously looking around.

"Shut the damn door!" McBride called.

Joyce shut it and followed Brown in from the foyer, leaving Angus near the foot of the stairs.

Brown took the reading chair near the front window and Joyce came stupidly to a stop between the back of the couch and the kitchen sink like he'd just lost a round of musical chairs.

"Help yourselves to goblets of coffee," McBride said to everyone.

"Goblets?" said Sylvia.

"Are you going to call him?" Brown said.

Sylvia picked up her phone from the table, causing a stir.

"Everybody calm down," McBride said. "It's just an iPhone."

"You said *you* were going to call him," Joyce said.

"He doesn't take my calls anymore." To Brown: "You both mistrust me because you both think I'm working for the other one. It's like a hall of mirrors. Isn't it ironic?"

Sylvia tapped her phone a few times and put it back down on the table.

"Well?" Brown said.

"I texted him."

"Did he respond?"

"Not yet."

"Everybody just take a pill," McBride said. "It's not the spy who came in from the cold here. It's just our little coffee klatsch. What shall we do to pass the time? How about a game of strip poker? Mike, I think there's a deck of unmarked cards in the drawer of the pantry there. Who hasn't seen who naked yet?"

"The more you joke," Brown said, "the more absurd you become."

"I haven't seen you in the buff yet, John, but I've seen your double — we both have — so that's almost as good. Mike, you don't get to play."

"Did he respond?" Brown said to Sylvia.

"Not yet."

"Thirty seconds, and I'm leaving."

"It will take him a few minutes."

"Why?"

"What's the rush?" McBride said. "Give him time to get over here."

"He hasn't even responded to her message."

"So what? He was expecting it. Give him five minutes. His driver is probably stuck in morning traffic."

Brown was as nervous as a perp waiting on his jury to come in. He couldn't sit back in his seat. He kept looking over at Joyce. Joyce kept watching McBride. Sylvia sat with her long legs stretched out and crossed in front of her, cool as ice.

McBride had never seen Sylvia like this before. She looked completely relaxed and completely alert, like a lion tamer surrounded by frustrated cats. Something was up that she hadn't told him. It gave him a hollow feeling. He tried not to show it. But he was getting the shakes.

A minute crept by. Another minute.

Brown thrust himself up. "Fuck it. That's enough."

"He's on his way," McBride said.

"Fuck it."

McBride and Sylvia got up.

Brown headed out into the foyer. They all rolled up behind him. Joyce passed ahead to get the door. Angus stepped aside to cover the rear.

McBride and Sylvia were just through the door into the foyer and Joyce, to their left, was just opening the front door, when, to their right, the back door banged open behind Angus, and Morris Gray leapt inside. Everybody, even Sylvia, jumped. Gray was still wearing the Bruins jersey and blue jeans, though most of the face paint had worn off, and he was soaking wet, and pale beneath the remaining splotches and streaks of black and gold paint, and he had a very small gun in his right hand, one of those little 9mm pocket-rockets.

•   •   •

A lot of things happened very quickly.

McBride yelled, "Gun!"

Brown was at the opposite end of the foyer from Gray and everybody but Joyce was between them in the narrow space. Gray had the gun pointed in Brown's direction but he didn't have a clear shot — and didn't fire to clear the way, thank God.

Angus whirled around but stumbled over Sylvia's feet and missed his grab for Gray's gun.

Gray ducked right, seeking a line on Brown.

Joyce wheeled and hurled Brown behind him in one big move that threw them both off balance.

McBride dropped to one knee as he reached for his own gun under his arm.

Sylvia, however, had turned in front of him toward Gray. She shouted, "Morris!" and stepped toward him.

Gray looked past her, focusing on Brown. The stairs to the upper floor rose from Gray's right and he darted up a couple of steps, seeking an angle. But he was right-handed so he had to lean over the rail to aim at Brown.

McBride had a shot at Gray now but he hesitated to kill him — he felt Brown behind him pinned against the safest corner, below the stairs. Gray was bumbling on the stairs, and Sylvia was striking out at him. There was a chance of hitting her instead.

Angus, getting his feet under him again, lunged at Gray, and instead collided with Sylvia, who was reaching over the bottom of the stair rail for Gray's gun hand.

McBride saw on his left another gun appear. It was Joyce, behind him, drawing down on Gray. McBride jumped up, flinging his left arm up to deflect Joyce's shot, and driving backwards to knock him down. He was almost too late. Joyce's shot exploded in his ear but passed above Gray and Sylvia and cut into the pine paneling beyond them.

Angus's collision with Sylvia made her miss her grab at Gray and Gray got off a shot. This second bang was also spectacularly loud in the small paneled space, like a thunderclap inside a cave.

Gray didn't miss his mark by much. The slug whacked into the door frame just inches wide of Brown's face.

Joyce and McBride tumbled backwards off their feet. With his free hand Joyce reached around and tried to yank McBride's chin into the next room. Hitting the wall broke the maneuver but hurt them both.

Brawls in both ends of the foyer.

Brown's paralysis broke. He started yelling wordlessly.

Before Gray could steady his hand to pull off another try at Brown, Sylvia had his wrist — reaching across his back with her left hand she yanked his gun hand up and back, twisting his arm out.

Gray let out a yelp of pain and tried to hold on to the gun and clenched off another deafening shot that went through the ceiling at the top of the stairwell. Plaster and splinters powdered down like shattered birds.

McBride came down on his back on top of Joyce. Both men still had guns in their right hands. Joyce tried to club McBride with the butt of his. McBride ducked into the blow to lessen it but it still stunned him.

Sylvia used Gray's arm like a lever to drive him face-down onto the uncarpeted stairs, stumbling over his feet and the steps as she did it, and letting herself come down hard on top of him. The breath whumped out of him but he kept hold of his weapon. She got both her hands on his gun hand and yanked his thumb back to open his grip. The little pistol came free and clattered down the stairs.

Brown screamed louder, hysterical, incoherent, but having the general effect of yelling "Sic 'em!" to a guard dog.

McBride used the back of his head to smash Joyce's nose. Joyce grunted and McBride rolled off of him.

Sylvia sprawled on top of Gray on the stairs.

Angus, trying to get to Gray, reached down and grabbed a fistful of McBride's over-sized sweatshirt on Sylvia's back and heaved her bodily into the air.

Out of control, she slammed into the wall facing the foot of the stairs like a sack full of angry timber rattlers.

Gray squirmed on the stairs, trying to retrieve his gun, which was at Angus's feet now, and Angus pounded a sledgehammer blow into the side of his head.

Gray grunted in a sickening way and curled up.

McBride and Joyce, both stunned and faces bloody, fought on their knees. Joyce, leaning on his gun hand, clubbed McBride with his left. McBride ducked away but took a glancing blow to the side of head. Bringing his right hand after him he clocked Joyce square in the temple with the butt of his Walther.

Angus was drawing his arm back to deliver Gray a finishing blow when Sylvia struck back. She punched him hard in the kidneys from behind and he gasped and choked on his breath and before he had time to get his huge bulk turned toward her she stomped on his right knee bending it sideways and he dropped off his feet like a building shortened by a demolition blast and started to fall over. He was going for his gun as he fell, and she saw it and dropped her knee into his ribs, using the momentum of her body mass to drive him down harder. His head banged into the bottom step, and he went out, his gun half drawn.

Joyce tottered back on his knees, dazed by McBride's pistol butt. His hands lost their way and struck out weakly as he sank back on his heels.

McBride punched him one more time out of spite, and his nose, already bleeding, broke across the bridge. He fell over like a Norway pine with a hip fracture.

Sylvia snatched up Angus's gun and swept Gray's away from him.

Gray, still half-conscious, lay pathetically squirming, his legs pinned under Angus's dead weight.

McBride pulled Joyce's gun from his slack hand, then hauled himself onto the bench under the stairs like he was going to take his boots off.

Brown had stopped screaming "Kill him!" or whatever it was he had been shrieking. He stood in the corner by the open front door, pale and shaking, glaring down at Joyce trying to lift himself up and at McBride slumped forward on the bench, blood dripping from the cut on his cheek.

Through the door McBride saw the driver and Cora running up the driveway from the black Suburban. You had to admire Brown's people's training.

CHAPTER 62

THE PREPONDERANCE
OF THE SMALL

The driver stopped at the threshold, stunned by the scene. Beside him Brown stood pale, trembling, speechless. At his feet Joyce was groaning on hands and knees, trying to find a way to his feet. McBride sat up on the bench and asked with a look whether the driver was going to be another problem. He wasn't. At the far end of the foyer Sylvia stood in McBride's baggy clothes like some comic book heroine, legs apart, guns in either hand, eyes ablaze, two semi-conscious men sprawled at her feet.

"You all right, boss?" said the driver.

Brown nodded, seeking for his voice, found it, and choked out, "Get the car ready."

"Yes, sir."

"Take Mike outside."

Stooping, the driver helped Joyce get up. Joyce resisted leaving, trying to look back at McBride.

"Go on, Mike," Brown said, touching his shoulder.

He went, dizzily, relying on the driver to keep him from weaving.

Sylvia stepped outside and put the two guns on the table between the Adirondack chairs. Then came back inside and helped Gray sit up. He leaned against the wall, hugging his right arm. His right cheek was livid and swelling.

Angus, like a sparrow recovering from a picture window, was trying shakily to lift himself up too, but his right knee wasn't going to take any weight.

McBride said, "Cora! Can you help this idiot out?"

Cora appeared in the doorway. Her eyes met Sylvia's and slid away. McBride nodded toward Angus, who'd propped himself up to one elbow so far.

"He'll need a doctor," Sylvia said, and there was a vicious little triumph in her voice.

Brown nodded assent, and Cora went to Angus and helped him pull himself up while Sylvia stood by, guarding Gray.

Cora helped Angus hobble to the front door. As they passed him Brown said, "Cora, take him to the emergency room in Mike's truck. We'll bring Mike with us."

"OK."

McBride stood unsteadily and closed the door after them. "Now let's all limp into the living room and have a grown-up conversation."

To McBride's surprise, Brown took his elbow to support him.

Sylvia helped Gray get up and go in.

Brown collected a dishtowel from the kitchen and gave it to McBride to stanch his cheek.

Gray settled down on the couch in the center of the room, looking frail and sick. Sylvia, McBride, and Brown resumed their previous seats, surrounding him.

Nobody spoke for a minute. Gray began quietly to cry, the tears further smearing his tattered face paint.

Through the window McBride watched Cora help Angus drag his leg into the passenger side of Joyce's truck, then get in herself and drive off.

Gray spoke, his voice a raw whisper: "I have failed."

Brown glared at him. "What's wrong with you?"

Gray raised his eyes from the floor. "You know."

"You can't kill me," Brown said. It was a plea, not a boast.

"Somebody will."

Brown could not respond. Fear and anger distressed his face in waves.

"Why?" McBride said. "What's going on?"

"He knows," Gray said.

"Well, I don't. Tell me."

"We're not brothers. We're not twins."

"You're not?"

"No, we're the same person."

Brown stomped the floor in frustration.

"You're the same person?" McBride said.

"Yes."

"In two bodies?"

"No."

"Is there another one? Maybe you're a trinity."

"We came here from the future."

Brown started. "I told you he was nuts!" he shouted.

"He came first," Gray said heavily. "Then they sent me to stop him."

"Now you believe me? He needs help."

"All right," McBride said, kindly, to Gray. "Well, we'll see. You should get to a hospital though. You look bad."

Gray gasped a little. His eyes wandered off, as though lost in grief. "It doesn't matter now," he said. "It's over for me."

The way he looked now, the way he spoke, was hair-raising. McBride had once tried to talk down a suicide who spoke like that —just before he jumped. And then you're standing there alone and confused because an entire human being has suddenly vanished out of the world.

Gray leaned over, and at first McBride thought he was passing out, but he was just reaching for the back pocket of his jeans.

Thinking it was another gun, McBride grabbed his up from where he'd laid it on the table beside him.

But it was a little book. He held it out to Sylvia. "Here," he said. "I want you to have this."

She bent forward to take it. It was the book of nature poetry that he'd bought the first day they'd spent together, and read to her as they sat on the bench in Boston Common.

McBride put the gun back down on the table, but Gray started fishing into another pocket and came up with a small object, which he handed over to McBride. It was a transparent hard-rubber ball, about the size of a golf ball.

"What's this?" McBride said.

"It's my report. It's the last thing I want to hire you for. I want you to take it out and drop it in the ocean. They'll find it. They're waiting for it."

"For God's sake, McBride," Brown said, with more desperation than pity.

"It's a kid's toy bouncer," McBride said.

"It's not supposed to look like anything important," Gray said wearily. "I left the money in Sylvia's living room. All the money, not just what I owe you, more, all I have left. It's on the ugly leather chair."

"Morris," Sylvia said softly, choked up.

He looked at her, tears welling in his eyes. He looked at McBride. "Thank you both," he said, his voice pitiful and chilling. He turned away and looked at Brown. "I failed," he said.

Brown appealed to McBride, but said nothing.

Gray looked back at Sylvia again, his face ghastly.

"They said it wouldn't hurt," he said, his eyes going white, and then he sucked in a ragged breath, and let it out again all at once, and slumped over on the couch, dead.

CHAPTER 63

AFTER COMPLETION

The next morning was chilly and grey. McBride found Sylvia sitting on the porch, wrapped in a blanket, warming her hands around a cup of coffee. The ducks were quacking raucously from the lake. He lowered himself gingerly into the other chair. It felt especially hard today.

"Still sore?" she said.

"Aren't you?" His voice felt raw.

"Your cheek is really swollen."

"My left ear is still ringing." He stretched his jaw and tried unsuccessfully to shake the ring out. "How long have you been up?"

"An hour or so."

"How's your back?"

"Hurts like hell. I wonder if I cracked a rib."

"You were spectacular, by the way."

"Was I?"

"You're the only reason the body count wasn't higher. My plan was to just shoot everybody and call it a day." He saw his shell lying on the shore below the yard where Gray had left it when he rowed over from Sylvia's. "Forgot to bring my boat up last night."

"I didn't know Morris had a gun. Really."

"Did you go by your place on your run?"

"No, why? Oh, the money?"

"What shall we do with it?"

"Fifty-fifty."

"No, I mean, I was thinking we should do something with it."

"Spend it?"

"I was thinking maybe we could take a cruise."

"You mean, together?"

He gave her a malevolent look, but she was smiling.

"Where to?" she said.

"Wherever the first ship out of Boston is going this morning. And then from there to some other damn place."

"The cops said they wanted us to stay in town for questioning."

"We always say that."

The police had been there most of the rest of the day, interrogating the five of them, examining the bullet holes in the doorjamb, wall, and ceiling, and searching the house for God knows what. McBride hadn't met any of them personally before, but he knew how to talk the talk, which was all that kept everybody from going in for still more questioning. Brown's attorney was on site even before the cops got there and helped McBride finesse the Q&A like a master. They gave the OIC a more or less plausible version of events of recent days, leaving out the craziest parts of the story and the satchel of cash. Eventually the cops got bored and lost interest. The EMTs zipped Brown's alter ego into a body bag and hauled it off to the coroner. Brown and his entourage filed out to the black Suburban.

"When do you want to go?" Sylvia said.

"As soon as I finish this coffee."

"Do we get to pack?"

"Passport, credit card, go."

"Cell phone?"

"Fuck no."

"What about this?" Gray's rubber ball was sitting like an oversize ice cube in a dry martini glass on the table between their chairs. Neat. Like he'd just learned a new word. "I noticed you didn't mention it to the cops yesterday."

"You don't think that's why I suggested taking a cruise, do you?"

"Of course not."

"Good."

"But let's bring it with us anyway."

CHAPTER 64

BEFORE COMPLETION

They found a "last-minute getaway" deal on a ship leaving late that afternoon, the Holland America *Tweelingdam*. They had just enough time to split up the cash and get it in the bank, pack a change of clothes, button up their dwellings and vehicles, and cab into Seaport to spend two hours queuing and jostling with a thousand tourists in the cavernous Cruiseport terminal. The fat white cruiser lay berthed beyond the glass wall like some misplaced Atlantic City casino had somehow washed up in Boston Harbor.

They had an overpriced stateroom with two beds and a balcony, but they spent the first evening lounging on the aft promenade, watching the lights of the New World sink over the horizon. The sea air turned fresh and they covered up with blankets and napped between rounds of strawberry daiquiris until the night grew very late and they were alone on the deck. The churn of the ship's wake stretched away like a gravel lane, smoldering white. A potbelly moon lit the broken clouds with silver fire. A catching breeze tousled their hair at intervals.

Sylvia said, "When do you want to do it?"

McBride suppressed his first reply. He was that tired and sore. "Do what?"

"The ball."

"You have it now?"

"In my pocket." She felt her jacket to confirm. In the opposite pocket, *The Sky Is Higher Than You Think, The Earth Is Lower Than You Know.*

"You don't think it's real," he said. More imperative than inquiry.

"Anything's possible."

"Not really."

"Why can't it be possible?" She sounded annoyed.

"Because if it's possible to travel into the past then causality must be an illusion. If causality is an illusion then nothing is sure. Detectives can't detect because nothing causes anything. Clues aren't clues. Logic isn't logic. Guilt isn't guilt."

"How do you know that isn't the case? There's no way to know."

"If that is the case then nothing is the case. Then there's no way to establish that anything is ever the case. Then the world is really actually an illusion, not just in philosophers' dreams."

"I can deal with that."

"It's not your illusion. It's not your choice."

"How would you know? How do you know you're not a butterfly dreaming you're a man? How do you know I'm not a Hindu goddess and you're not some weirdo in a nightmare I'm having?"

"I don't. But I do know how the rules work in this dream."

"Do you? Maybe you just ignore what doesn't suit your rules."

"Such as?"

"I don't know. It's lots of little things. Like when we saw the monkey in the Garden and he asked me if I thought it was real."

"He probably meant was it a pet or not."

"How do you know?"

"You think they don't have monkeys in the future?"

"At the rate we're killing everything off?" Point Sylvia.

But still. "Pretty thin, Syl."

"It's more about how he was. How he acted. His attitude toward everything. The McDonald's drive-thru was so cool. He was always out of sync somehow."

"Like he'd just arrived from the robot factory. You know, maybe that's it. Maybe Brown had a clone a spun up for a gag. Thing got lose and went rogue."

"And died." Darkly.

"Battery ran out."

"You're just being a jerk now."

"No I like this theory. Explains how he could drink so much. Good fuel source."

"I'm not going to let you piss me off tonight. But don't be like this the whole trip, OK? You might have an accident." She nodded toward the sea.

"Careful, partner. My mouth is a lethal weapon registered with the Commonwealth of Massachusetts."

"If shit could talk."

"It would talk about time travel."

Sylvia finished off her daiquiri and smacked it down hard on the little table between them. "You should hear yourself, McBee. You're ridiculous."

"All right. I'm sorry. I know you liked him. To be honest I liked him too in a way. More than I liked Brown anyway. But I just cannot take this seriously."

She got up and went for refills. The wait service had gone to bed. He watched her go — through the colored lights looped around the deck. Blue jeans and a black windbreaker. That athletic walk of hers. She swayed a little — from the daiquiris and the swell — but you could see in her hips that she could break you in half with her legs.

She returned three minutes later with daiquiris in either hand and the wind stole the umbrellas out of them and she put them on the table and pulled her blanket up again.

"It's getting pretty cold out here," she said.

"Cheers."

"So what killed him then?"

"Coroner will figure it out. Poisoned himself is my guess."

"Why would he?"

"Crazy."

"No."

"He told me he was going to die the first time I met him."

"A little crazy, sure. But crazy isn't the solution."

"It'll do."

"What about the photo?"

"It's a fake."

"Faked before it even happened?"

"None of us saw it happen."

"But you said—"

"Have you been to the movies lately? The stuff they can do with CGI now."

"You're not even trying to make ssense." She slurred a little, more cold than drunk.

"It can't be made to make sense. That's why it's impossible. I get paid to live in the logical world."

"Maybe the world isn't logical. Or not your kind of logic."

"I never made you for a Nietzschean."

"Well I think your attitude is what would make being a detective impossible. Because how could you learn anything really new? Anything that doesn't fit, you ignore. It's a ssealed system."

"And yet I am a detective."

"Because you don't really believe your own bullshit. It's just words, McBee. You need to take some real risks."

He twisted his finger in his ear. "My head is still ringing like a smoke alarm."

"Psychological risks. Put the philosophy away for a while. Write poetry."

"Roses are red. Violets are blue. I feel dizzy. What about you?"

"And let someone read it. That's the thing. I dare you to let someone read it."

There was feeling in her voice and it touched him. *Dare.* "OK."

"OK what?" She didn't trust him.

"OK I take your point. OK I know I've been a surly bastard for a long time. OK I don't have much of a life really."

"I'm not trying to beat up on you."

"You suggested I might go overboard."

"Well I'd probably feel bad about it and throw you a lifesaver."

"Thanks, pal."

"But seriously. Lighten up."

"Yes, ma'am." He pulled his blanket off and sat up facing her. "Speaking of going overboard. Let's do the thing."

They stood and stepped to the aft rail.

Sylvia took the ball from her pocket and gave it to him. "You do the honors."

McBride held it up like an old coin and they both examined it again. The clear plastic caught the colorful deck lights internally. You could almost imagine it was some kind of device. Two for a buck at Dollar General.

He palmed it again. "Well, here's to Morris Gray. Whoever you were. Wherever you came from. You were one or two of a kind." He drew back and hurled the ball away. It was lost in the darkness and moon-glimmer before it splashed.

Sylvia waved once. "Goodbye, Morris."

The deck lifted and rolled and Sylvia leaned against him and put her arm around his waist. He put his around her. They watched the sea-lane churn away. Fire on the water.

"Well this is romantic," he said.

"I'm not sad though," she said.

He thought of their first sit-down with Brown, watching the Suburban drive off down A Street. Not so much as a parking ticket on Brown. Data point.

Acknowledgments

I am indebted to a number of people for feedback, encouragement, and inspiration, without whom this book, such as it is, would have been less: Brock Clarke, the Colgate Writers Conference, Marya Spont-Lemus, Lauren Baratz-Logsted, Kat Warren, Paul Clark.

About the Author

Gary Glass wrote his first novel over monsoon season in the Himalayas. He has been an ad writer in Taiwan, a racehorse exerciser in Japan, a NICU registered nurse in Indiana. He spent a summer riding the rails across the United States. He's also a lifelong photographer and has a software engineering patent. In addition to two previous novels, he has published short fiction, poetry, and essays. He currently lives with his wife in Valencia, Spain, where he's working on his fourth book.

Note from the Author

Word-of-mouth is crucial for any author to succeed. If you enjoyed *The Brothers Brown and Gray*, please leave a review online—anywhere you are able. Even if it's just a sentence or two. It would make all the difference and would be very much appreciated.

Thanks!
Gary Glass

We hope you enjoyed reading this title from:

www.blackrosewriting.com

Subscribe to our mailing list – *The Rosevine* – and receive **FREE** books, daily deals, and stay current with news about upcoming releases and our hottest authors.
Scan the QR code below to sign up.

Already a subscriber? Please accept a sincere thank you for being a fan of Black Rose Writing authors.

View other Black Rose Writing titles at www.blackrosewriting.com/books and use promo code **PRINT** to receive a **20% discount** when purchasing.

www.ingramcontent.com/pod-product-compliance
Lightning Source LLC
Chambersburg PA
CBHW010730100726

47899CB00009B/2999